99 LT

M

KILLERS' HARVEST

A money man and a law deputy were murdered and a girl taken hostage by four badmen who went on the run. But they failed to reckon on veteran gunfighter Jay Lessiter, or on Goldie Santono's bandidos. And so it all flared up into a vicious feud of blood and greed casting its onerous shadow across the borderlands. Few would escape death before the guns ceased firing and peace returned.

Books by Vic J. Hanson
in the Linford Western Library:

KILLER ALONE
SILVO

VIC J. HANSON

KILLERS'
HARVEST

Complete and Unabridged

LINFORD
Leicester

First published in Great Britain in 1996 by
Robert Hale Limited
London

First Linford Edition
published 1997
by arrangement with
Robert Hale Limited
London

British Library CIP Data

Hanson, Vic J.
    Killers' harvest.—Large print ed.—
Linford western library
1. Western stories
2. Large type books
I. Title
823.9'14 [F]

ISBN 0–7089–5127–9

Published by
F. A. Thorpe (Publishing) Ltd.
Anstey, Leicestershire
Set by Words & Graphics Ltd.
Anstey, Leicestershire
Printed and bound in Great Britain by
T. J. International Ltd., Padstow, Cornwall

This book is printed on acid-free paper

For Joan and George Boulton

1

"HE'S an old-stager," said Kellern. "An old war-dog. Hell, although he was reputed to be good in his time, them days are long gone."

"He was supposed to be the fastest draw in a lot o' territory," said Rollo doubtfully.

"Fast ain't allus accurate," said Kellern.

"Yeh, I heard he got shot bad," said Little Cass brightly. "I heard he's got a mighty bad shoulder, his right 'un, an' that he'd never been a two-gun man."

The fourth man hadn't said anything, although Kellern had looked at him a couple of times as if soliciting his approval. A taciturn half-breed was Deegon, and that wasn't his real name anyway. He'd lived with both

1

the Apaches and their enemies, the Comanches. Later, in his adulthood, he'd run with the polyglot *comancheros*, the renegade scum of the borderlands.

"One of us should've gone in first," said Rollo, who worried at things like a cur dog with a smelly rag. "Taken an eyeful of that ol' law-dog. Two-gun or no two-gun, he's a veteran who's still toting a law-badge, so he's gotta be good at somep'n."

"Drunk-baiting I guess," said Kellern scornfully.

"Anyway, I didn't want anybody to see any of us, if y'see what I mean. Am I organizing this job or ain't I?"

He looked at his longest-time partner, Rollo, who was of about his own age, thirtyish, dark, poker-faced, clean-shaven, his thin hair hidden under a big hat.

Rollo said, "Yeh, we all agreed you'd fix the job. Let's get on with it then."

Neither Little Cass or Deegon made any comment, and Kellern said, "Hold your hosses. We'll go in by night.

2

The light's failin' already. We'll hunker down in that little draw ahead an' wait."

He led the way and only the chink of bridles and the soft thud of slow hooves disturbed the quiet night.

He dismounted and they followed their leader's example. He was the tallest, quiet-looking, sporting a lush black moustache that made him look older than his years. There was a lot of black hair on his head also, worn long beneath his Stetson, past the brim and almost to his shoulders.

A natty dresser whenever possible, cheerful, intelligent, hiding his inherent ruthlessness under a smiling mask, his white teeth (he cleaned them with a peeled stick like an Indian) gleaming beneath the facial adornment on his otherwise clean-shaven visage.

Rollo passed makings around and they all lit up. At least, three of them did. The fourth, Deegon, lay flat on his back, pulled his sombrero over his eyes and went to sleep. He wasn't as big as Kellern or Rollo and, as he was now, he looked puny. But, if awakened suddenly, he could strike like a sidewinder.

Little Cass was no bigger than Deegon, though considerably younger. Twenty and tow-headed, with a pale, straggly moustache which didn't make him look any older. Still boyish-looking, he had an uncertain temper and a fast gunhand, Kellern kept an eye on him. Cass, leaning on a smooth rock now, smoking, watched the town ahead as the night began to take over and the lights winked on.

* * *

Deputy Steal didn't see Curly Bess every night, only four times a week at most, but he was as regular as clockwork. He'd been upstate on an errand for the marshal and hadn't seen Bess for nigh on a week, and that was mighty unusual. Crossing the deserted street to the front of the bordello, he

4

hastened his steps, knowing Bess would be waiting for him as he'd managed to get word to her via a potman earlier that day.

In the dimly shaded lobby he saw the madam, who came from Kansas City and called herself Drusilla. She bade him 'good evening' offhandedly, and he went up the stairs.

Bess had heard him coming and when he entered her small but comfortable, poorly lit room she was lying on the bed waiting, wearing only her bright red and blue moccasins.

"Quiet as a grave out there," he said.

"I missed you, honey," she said.

After that, they didn't talk much.

He always came in by the front, not by the backstairs like most of the other visitors. The marshal knew of his passion for Curly Bess. The town knew; and it was an easygoing town. Young Tim Steal wanted to marry Curly Bess and make a good woman of her, but a deputy marshal's pay was meagre and Bess made a lot more than he did. So time went on and in Tim's eyes Bess didn't become any less beautiful. He was good at his job and his chief, Marshal Lessiter, was easy with him, was taking the night shift in the jailhouse now because the old jailer, Saul, was in bed with croup.

After his travels, Tim had had a good sleep. But he knew that the marshal had had a long hard day and would want to get his head down now, so Tim didn't stay too long with Bess and left Drusilla's place, known by some as the Dally House, by the front and crossed the street towards the law office.

There was nobody about. But then he heard a scuffle behind him, past the Dally House. He turned and he saw the two men. Curious, he walked towards them.

He didn't hear the approach of the third man till that man was right behind him, and then he turned about again, reaching for his gun.

The knife went deeply into his side, high up, near the heart. The man's free hand gripped Tim's shoulder and forced him on to his knees as he died, his gun unsheathed, a sound expelling from his lips, a high wail which died with a choking sob.

There wasn't much light near the whorehouse. Bess, looking from her window, trying to watch her lover as he left her, didn't see much, just a cluster of figures. But she heard that horrid cry. Dressed as she was then, in a flimsy shift, she ran downstairs and out into the street.

There were three men by the huddled body of Deputy Marshal Tim Steal, and a fourth man was leading horses forward. Bess screamed.

"Take her," one of the men said.

She screamed again and turned towards the dimly lit doorway she had just left. She heard thudding bootheels behind her and then her small body was grabbed around the waist and a big hand clamped her mouth, stifling her. She was only vaguely aware of the smell of a horse as she was thrown across a saddle, and then she lost consciousness.

2

FOLKS came running from the front of the whorehouse. There was no concealment now. Folks came running down the street too, and somebody yelled something about 'a robbery'. There was turmoil.

Folks gathered around the huddled form of Deputy Tim Steal. There was nothing they could do for him. The madam, Drusilla, was shouting something about Curly Bess. Her half-dressed girls were skittering like so many chickens with their heads chopped off.

Two men ran for the law office but before they reached it, Marshal Jay Lessiter could be seen coming out, buckling on his gunbelt, shouting questions in that deep, authoritative voice of his, folks yelling answers — and there were the many questioners also. And nothing making much sense.

Jay Lessiter got down on one knee beside the body of his deputy, his young partner and friend who had been like a cheerful son to him.

"Horsemen rode out," said somebody. "Four of 'em. They'd got the girl with them."

"Curly Bess," shrilled Madam Drusilla. "They took Curly Bess."

"Marshal," said a male voice. "The express office has been robbed. Pete Dromwell's been killed."

Jay Lessiter rose slowly to his feet. "Look after Tim," he said. There were willing hands.

Jay pulled himself erect as he followed a few more people down the street towards the express office. He was a big man and heavier than he used to be. He was bareheaded and his thick hair was black with wings of grey over his ears. He wore a moustache which he trimmed now more than he used to. He wasn't the show-off pistoleer that he once was.

Although he didn't look it, he was

forty-eight years old, which was kind of long in the tooth for a serving marshal in a town that was no better than it should be. He wore togs that could best be described as range clothes but, with that, the description ended. He wore one gun — he'd pouched it now — in a holster not too low-slung and a bit more forward from his hip than was usual, ideal for a conventional draw with the right hand or a cross-arm one with the left.

The door of the express office was wide open and a woman leaned in a slumped position beside it, her face in her hands, her slim shoulders shaking as she wept brokenly.

Marshal Lessiter caught her arm gently. "Come inside, Martha," he said. "Come on, honey."

She let him lead her into the light of the suspended lanterns where the local doctor was already rising from the body of her husband.

"Nothing I can do, Jay, I'm almighty sorry."

So the marshal's informant had been right. Express agent Pete Dromwell, who was a little younger than the lawman, had been battered around the head, his face twisted, mutilated. Men — five of them now counting the doc — shielded the corpse from Martha Dromwell's gaze.

Jay Lessiter led her to a wooden armchair with cushions upon it and sat her down. She was a well-shaped, pretty, brown-haired woman, younger than her husband had been. Now her face was red and swollen from weeping and her eyes were glazed.

Doc Swan approached her, said, "You should get to bed, Martha. I'll give you something."

"I want to stay here," she said and suddenly, as she looked up at him, her eyes were clearer. Her voice was steady as she went on, "I might be able to help. I saw one of them. There were four, and I didn't see the other three. But I saw one of them pretty clearly."

12

Doc turned, called, "Jay." And the marshal joined them, moving quickly and very lightly, his blue eyes sharp, direct.

"Can you talk, Martha?"

"I can talk, Jay." They were carrying the body of her husband to the marriage bed they had shared for a score of years. She'd been only seventeen when she married Pete. It had been a sometimes stormy passage and they had no children.

* * *

"We got what we went for anyway," said Rollo. Though Kellern's main and oldest partner, he was always the argumentative one.

"It could've been better though, like I said," affirmed Kellern. "I didn't plan for no killing. And Cass shouldn't have battered that clerk the way he did."

"He came at me like a madman," said Little Cass. "He wouldn't let go. And Deegon had to stop that other

13

feller too. He wore a star, wuz a lawman or somep'n."

"That wasn't the old dog lawman you were talkin' about, was it?" said Rollo, looking at his partner.

"Must've been a deputy," said Kellern.

Deegon, as usual, said nothing. By his lights it had been a sweet job.

The girl was over the front of Rollo's saddle and she was still unconscious. "Did you hit her with somep'n?" Cass demanded.

"No, she just passed out. What're we gonna do with her?"

"She's our hostage," said Kellern. "She might come in useful for somethin'."

"Come to think of it," said Rollo, chuckling, "I reckon I could use her well for something."

"She came outa that whorehouse," said Cass. "I see'd that. You could catch somep'n."

"How'd you know it was a whore-house?"

"Hell, I could tell. It was obvious."

"Little Cass is a sort of authority on whorehouses," said Kellern.

Suddenly, the small young feller seemed to take this remark as a compliment. "I'm careful," he said. "And now Rollo's given me an idea."

"I should've killed the woman like I killed that deputy," said Deegon suddenly and they all looked at him with a kind of astonishment; they were struck speechless. They rode, the sack with the money in it over the front of Kellern's saddle and lashed safely with rawhide.

The girl began to moan. She twisted on the saddle and, in the light from the pale moon, Rollo could see her face.

"She's a purty little thing," he said.

"Gag her," said Kellern and Rollo took his bandanna from his neck.

"There are ranches nearby," Kellern explained. "I saw 'em when I came by before. There could be cattle an' night riders."

Nobody argued with him. They could see small lights in the distance. They knew Kellern had passed this way and none of them had till earlier this night. And Kellern had got his information about new boodle waiting in the express office. His informant hadn't mentioned how conscientious was the express man, how aggressive also.

"How about your friend Andy then?" said Rollo waspishly.

Andy was an old boyhood acquaintance of Kellern's who had sort of turned up out of nowhere a few weeks ago. Rollo had met him once and hadn't liked him, hadn't trusted him, although he had to admit to himself now that the information that Andy had given to Kellern had been correct.

"Andy will catch up with us," Kellern said. "He'll get a rig an' the train. His leg an' all, y'know."

"We could hit the border an' never see him again," said Little Cass.

"Don't talk like an idiot," said Kellern. "He knows us. We don't want to hafta keep runnin'. Besides, I gave him my word."

Rollo began to laugh mockingly. But then the girl struggled, muffled sounds coming from behind her gag, and he had to pay her more attention, grasp her tightly as he said, "Keep still an' quiet, little lady, or I'll have to throw you down on the ground an' stomp you. But if you're good I'll treat you nice, I promise."

She became still and silent but, in a little while, Rollo asked her for her name, pulling her gag down, raising a warning finger.

"They call me Curly Bess," she whispered.

"Purty," said Rollo. "Listen, I'm gonna take this thing off your mouth but if you raise your voice or try anything funny I'll hand you over to my little pard," — he jerked his head in the direction of Deegon — "an' you saw how he handled that boy back in town, didn't you?"

She nodded her head, wordlessly, and he removed the gag. The others glanced at him, hard, but nobody said anything. There were no lights now, no sound except the steady thud of hooves. There were a few stars high in the heavens and the pale slice of moon shone benignly on the four men and the captive girl as they went steadily on their way.

3

"IT was the one who killed Pete," said Martha. "He was young and quite small. Looked like a boy but acted like a maniac, kept beating at Pete with the barrel of his gun. One of the others called him, a tall one, but he didn't turn round, so I didn't see his face. But the young one turned on me and I thought he was goin' to shoot me. But then he looked sort of dazed and he turned and went after the others who'd already disappeared through the door . . . I had no gun, Pete had no gun, he'd just — just sat up, watching. He always behaved like that when we had a lot of money here. It was to be picked up in the morning . . . "

"I know," put in Marshal Jay Lessiter, giving her a rest as her voice became broken. "And Pete was good at his job, and a man with guts

19

also, the way he tried to stand up to that scum."

"Martha started to yell an' I came here," said another man, the informant who had accosted the marshal in the street as he rose from the body of Deputy Tim Steal. The man lived next door to the express office, a widower on his own. He had seen the four horsemen ride out but hadn't been able to get a good look at any of them, hadn't had a gun with him either so hadn't been able to get in a shot, a fact he bemoaned now.

"You couldn't know what was happening," Jay Lessiter told him, knowing, as the others did, that Martha and Pete had often fought and hadn't always been quiet about it.

Doc Swan had gone. Another man was outside, acting on the marshal's instructions, getting a posse together. They began to shout outside. There was the clatter of hooves. "I'll be all right, Jay," said Martha, and he left her.

But she called him back as he was going through the door.

"That one I saw — who was struggling with Pete. I remember what he looked like — except he was so young of course. I'm sorry . . . "

"Take your time, honey," Lessiter said.

Her fine eyes were wide with strain. But her voice was more level when she went on, "He had tow hair, and a wispy sort of moustache. Yellow . . . Like he was trying to make himself look older. But it didn't work. He was like a crazy boy. I thought he was going to shoot me . . . till the other called him, spoke his name. Like a girl's name . . . "

Her eyes became clouded with the pain and the effort. But then they lightened.

"Cass," she cried. "The other man called him Cass."

"Got it," said Lessiter. "Can you . . . ?"

"Here's Lily. She'll look out for

her." Lily was her elder sister, bustling through the door now, anxious, but eminently capable, saying "Hello, Jay" as he passed her.

"Lil," he said. Then he was with the posse, and one of its members brought the marshal's horse forward saddled and ready.

They knew which way the killers had gone. The posse had sorted itself well. All good men. Seven strong now, counting their leader, Marshal Jay Lessiter.

Andy Lugo, limping out of the ever-open dairy with a pail of milk, watched them go and was fearful. It was time he went too. But would that be too soon? Would somebody maybe follow him? He couldn't wait too long. Kellern wouldn't wait forever, and probably his boys, particularly that slime, Deegon, would be pushing him.

It had seemed such a good plan, the one Andy and Kellern had cooked up. And there wouldn't have been a plan at all if it wasn't for Andy. Yes, it had been a good plan: he told himself this over and over.

But things had gone so terribly wrong!

He hadn't been afraid. He'd been cock-a-hoop. But now he was uncertain. Terribly, terribly uncertain.

For days beforehand Andy had known about the money that was coming to the express office from the mine miles away and would be there overnight until it was collected by a war-wagon the following morning.

It was a ploy of the mine-owners whose last shipment, conveyed straight from the mine to its destination, had been held up — and the bandits had escaped with a pile of money and vanished in the air it seemed. Nobody would have dreamed that this time the money would be taken by devious routes to a town miles away and actually left there overnight.

The money was for owners, shareholders, planners who had put their own money originally into the diggings in the hills, helping to turn them from the disused shambles that prospectors had given up on. There had been engineers, labourers, technicians. Deep, a new wide vein had been discovered. The speculators' gamble had succeeded and now they were being paid — in spades: the thought had amused Andy. Then by chance he'd met his old boyhood friend Kellern . . .

Nobody in town had been supposed to know about the shipment, except Pete Dromwell, and maybe his wife Martha.

But Pete, at the Dally House, and under the influence of booze and the practised charms of one of Drusilla's girls, had told bragging half-truths. And Andy, who flitted around the cathouse like a limping ghost had put two and two together and come up with five.

And the job had been done by Kellern, Rollo, Deegon and Little Cass.

Andy Lugo had wondered why, with a lovely wife like Martha, Pete spent so much time in the cathouse. But, even so, he hadn't wished Pete dead. Or Deputy Tim Steal, a likeable feller, if a mite too officious for Andy's taste. And Curly Bess had been kidnapped: that was the unkindest cut of all. Andy liked Curly Bess. He liked her very much. Soiled lady of the night though she was, Andy didn't like to think of her in the hands of such as Rollo, Deegon and the maniac, giggling Little Cass.

Maybe, once they were well on their way to freedom, and to the place where Andy had arranged to meet them, they would shoot Bess and dump her body. Andy didn't like to think of that possibility. Bess had been good to him.

She had never jeered at him because of his disability, as many of the other girls had. She had never struck him as Madam Drusilla had on many an occasion. When he had done little favours for her she had paid him well and had oftimes given him cigars and wine, but not so much of the latter because it made his head go funny.

Andy had sometimes told himself that were it not for Curly Bess he wouldn't stay at the cathouse, slavey that he was, not a favoured bully-boy like the other men Drusilla employed. He was a puny, crippled, unconsidered thing and the knowledge ate at him.

But what else could he find to do?

He had found something else he could do! He had a brain: he used it.

He made his way back to the house, trying not to spill milk from his pail. He squared his thin, narrow shoulders and picked the good parts of the street and sidewalk to favour his bad leg. And he began to use his brain again.

In the lobby big Drusilla scowled at him, asked him why he'd been so long. "Got held up, honey-bunch," he said, not telling her how that was. Her scowl deepened. She didn't like his being 'familiar' as she termed it. "Take that milk into the kitchen," she growled. "Then you can do the hall upstairs. It smells like a skunk."

"Yes, ma'am," he replied mockingly.

When he came back into the lobby there was nobody in sight. He got his broom and pail from under the stairs, figured he didn't need any water, just the pail for odd bits of rubbish. He didn't go back into the kitchen but climbed the stairs. When he was at the top a head with dishevelled hair popped out of a door to the left of him.

It was the yellow-haired filly called Pecos Lil whom the late express man, Pete Dromwell, had mightily fancied.

"C'mon in here, Andy."

He left his gear outside and followed the girl into the room. "Shut the door," she said and he kicked it to behind him. Then he saw the bare-chested man sitting on the bed and all his new thoughts and sassiness left him like so much pungent wind.

Andy had been scared of many things in his not too long life but this man, this *thing*, was the big item that he feared most of all.

"Hello, Andy," the man said.

"Hello, Goldie," said Andy weakly.

"I didn't expect to see you here again yet awhile." And that was a fact!

"Why not, Andy?" asked the man called Goldie. He had a silky voice with a nasty ring to it. "Why not yet awhile?"

"Oh, I dunno . . . " Andy was at a loss for words. His thoughts fled from him.

"Sit here next to me on the bed, Andy," said Goldie. "I have a few quiet questions I want to ask you."

Unspeaking, Andy joined him on the bed. Goldie looked at Pecos Lil and said, "Take a walk, honey. And keep your mouth shut."

He was dark and handsome and wore his black hair in a sort of pigtail. When he smiled you could see the gold tooth that had earned him his nickname. He had a long Mexican name and always claimed that his forebears were of aristocratic Spanish stock who could be traced back to the time of the Conquistadores.

The door closed behind Lil, and

Goldie said, "Take it easy, Andy. I'm not going to hurt you." But the small man was as taut now as an overwound spring threatening to split at any moment.

Goldie went on, "Only Lil and Drusilla know I'm here. And now you know. Isn't that something?"

"Yes, Goldie."

"Me and Lil have been having a talk, among other things. She tells me that that galoot who got himself killed down at the express office was a good friend of hers. Is that right, Andy? You'd know that wouldn't you, Andy? You know everything that goes on here, don't you, Andy? You listen at doors and peep through keyholes."

"No . . . Yes . . . "

"Make your goddamn mind up." Goldie's silky manner was suddenly violent. He gripped the top of Andy's damaged leg with the fingers of his big hand and he squeezed. The grip was like a vice and Andy gave a little involuntary cry of pain.

The well-built muscular man released his hold and said, "Listen to me good and don't give me any funny answers."

"I wasn't . . . " The grip was back, the pain.

"I'm listenin', Goldie."

"When I came into town I was surprised to learn there'd been trouble. I came in my usual way of course, this side and along the backs. I had to keep myself out of sight, didn't I, in case that goddamn marshal here figured I had something to do with that shindig? I heard from Drusilla and then I heard from Lil. I surely heard a lot from Lil, Andy. She knew that money was coming in because her friend, Pete, told her so. And you knew it too, didn't you, Andy?"

"No, I . . . "

"Don't lie to me or I'll break you in half. Lil reckons you must know. This room is at the top of the stairs and you know everything that goes on here. And you'll pass anything on you

30

learn if you think there's profit in it for you. So now, little *amigo*, you're going to pass what you know on to me. Profit or pain, little *amigo*. Death at the end. Or riches! Or maybe that was the plan after all, huh, you and your friends? But I'm your friend also, aren't I, Andy?"

He gave the boy a little nudge with his elbow and the boy said, "Yes, Goldie."

4

THE trail had gone cold and Marshal Jay Lessiter was way out of his jurisdiction. It was possible that the bunch of robbers and killers had gone over the border. This was wild and untracked territory.

Jay gave the word to turn back and it was obvious that the weary posse, which had ridden hard, was willing to do this. Some of its members made a token protest, but it was halfhearted. It was the first time that anything as bad as this had happened in their town, but they knew there was a good man at their head who knew what he was doing.

On the way back Jay was pretty silent. He was thinking hard, had to take a new tack.

When they reached town, he, like the others, washed up and got some sustenance. But he didn't rest. He changed his clobber, then he walked down to the Dally House, not a usual port of call for him.

He knew that Pete Dromwell had been a regular visitor there. That was no secret, not even from Pete's missus, Martha. And because Jay Lessiter had been Martha's old friend and, lately, her lover it had been no secret to him either.

Madam Drusilla was fidgety. She had some news for the law. Goldie Santono had been here and, when he left, he had taken young Andy with him.

"Which girl was Goldie with?"

"Pecos Lil."

"I'll go see her." He began to climb the stairs.

Drusilla called after him, "She's got a client."

He ignored this, rapped on the door at the lefthand side, top of the stairs.

There was no reply. But he could hear telling movements coming from behind the door. "Open up," he called.

There was a more frantic scuttle. Then the door opened and Pecos Lil stood there clad only in a flimsy shift, hastily donned, revealing a bare shoulder and part of a pendulous bub. Lil was no chicken, being possibly the Dally House's oldest girl, except for Drusilla of course, who didn't actually follow the profession nowadays, just managed it, and a martinet she was too.

Jay couldn't figure what a murderous fancy-pants like Goldie Santono could see in an old frail like Lil, though she was less than his (Jay's) own age. But I'm not a whore, he thought sardonically, and he said, "I want to talk to you privately," and pushed past her.

Lil's client was the local blacksmith, a widower, who, clad now in his wrinkled underdrawers which he'd obviously just pulled on, looked as big as a house.

"Sorry, Mike," said the marshal.

"That's all right, Jay. We'd finished

anyway. Did you ketch them bastards?"

"No, I'm afraid not, Mike."

The huge man was soon on his way. Lil, who had also quickly donned other, though flimsy, clothing, eyed the marshal with trepidation.

★ ★ ★

"He's late," said Rollo.

"He should be here any time now," said Kellern.

"We can't afford to wait," said Rollo.

"We'll wait a mite longer. I gave him my word."

"What do we do with her?" asked Little Cass, jerking a thumb in the direction of Curly Bess, who sat on the ground with her head sunk on her breast.

"I'll tell you later," said Kellern.

Back on the trail Little Cass had had the girl, and so had Rollo and Deegon. Kellern was the only one who'd abstained.

Little Cass strode over to the girl

35

now, reached down and grabbed her by the arm, said, "C'mon along o' me, *chiquita*."

"Leave her be," snapped Kellern. "I want you to keep your wits about you."

Cass whirled on him. "You're takin' too much on yourself, bucko," he snarled. "I'll use her if I want to, an' then I'll shoot her if I want to."

"I'll do what I want," said Kellern. "And you'll do what I want as well." His voice had gone softer, and now he spread his legs apart, held his hands away from his sides, his fingers spread, clawed at the ends.

"Goddammit," said Rollo. "We don't want any shootin'. We can't risk that."

He was right of course. "Later," said Little Cass.

"If you wish," said Kellern.

The four of them and the girl were in a long tumbledown shack on the edge of a settlement which had once been called Horsemen's Dip. The flatlands

36

behind it had been a popular place for sportsmen and gamblers from both sides of the border to run their fleet ponies and try their luck with plenty of green bills and gold coin.

There had been cockfighting there too, tuzzling canines, men confronting each other with stock-whips and knives, wrestling contests, and once an ex-circus man with a bear who would take on any number of snarling cur dogs and finally died of old age.

That had been in the old days, but now the place was little more than a ghost-town, the only occupants right now as far as the Kellern group could ascertain being a couple of half-crazy oldsters who prospected for gold in the hills a mile away on the North American side. Nobody had ever looked for gold there before. The two old crazies flitted from tumbledown ruin to tumbledown ruin and the boys hadn't been able to pin them down and Kellern said to leave 'em be, they'd cause no harm. This was an ideal rendezvous, Kellern said.

"Maybe that crooked little bastard has got himself lost," Rollo complained.

"Naw," said Kellern. "Andy knows this place well. He used to come here an' bet when he was just a kid, I've been with him a few times."

Deegon was asleep. The rest lay around and smoked. The girl seemed to be dozing. Nobody bothered her now. The sun came through cracks in the broken roof above them all.

Nobody was keeping watch now, but from time to time one of them rose and walked around the vantage points — and there were many — and took a look outside.

Lately nobody had spotted one of the old prospectors in the little ruined settlement or seen them leaving for the hills.

The group hadn't seen a posse, hadn't seen much at all before they got to this temporary hideout. Kellern had figured there had been a posse but they would have given up long since, them and that old law dog leading 'em.

"Deegon killed his deputy," Rollo had said.

"Deegon's got it in for lawmen," Kellern had said. "He'd kill the old 'un as well if he had a chance." And Deegon had nodded and chuckled and winked.

★ ★ ★

Santono, with Andy Lugo in tow, had joined the rest of Santono's boys at a place where they awaited their leader. Andy, bad leg or not, had been forced to ride a horse a long way and was immensely fatigued and bemused; wasn't so scared of the border mob as he might have expected to be.

That would come later. For Goldie Santono's border gang were the most cruel and ruthless killers, robbers, arsonists, torturers, rapists and kidnappers in any territory, more than a match for the law on both sides of the border or any marauding Apaches or Comanches.

There were a few renegade Apaches among them, and women too, Indian, white, or mixed. The nucleus of the band usually numbered about eight, counting the leader, comprising two Apaches, three Mexicans, though not high-born ones as Santono claimed to be, one half-breed and one Anglo. But Santono always had others on call if needs be, Anglo renegades and their *compadres* from over the border, wanted men and fugitives, the lowest scum of regions where standards were never very high anyway. These were folks who loved what they did, were full of greed and sadism and the lust to kill.

And the women on the sidelines picking up the scraps were no better than their men, among them two white girls who had escaped from Mexican bordellos, two split-nosed Apache squaws who had been mutilated and banished from their tribe, a

Mexican runaway with a hare lip and a maddeningly voluptuous body and a mulatto girl who had wandered in from nowhere, was a fine cook and spread her favours around as generously as she did her culinary delicacies.

Santono never availed himself of the fleshly charms of frails close to hand but went elsewhere. The band were glad to see him back, couldn't understand why he had toted a cripple boy back with him, and he didn't tell them why this was so. He told his favourites, all seven of 'em, to get mounted and he led them on.

The boy called Andy had been allowed to rest for a while but was made to mount up with the rest, and he rode side by side with the man called Goldie.

High-born though this man claimed to be he seemed to relish the nickname that Anglos had given to him, a name that had made him notorious and, more importantly, greatly feared.

Once he had had a travelling

photographer take his portrait festooned with armoury and looking like a handsome but also fearsome-looking, brigand. He had a Springfield rifle over his shoulder, twin Starr pistols at his hips, a bowie knife in an ornate scabbard and, crosswise across his chest, a wide bandolier with a full complement of cartridges.

On his head he'd worn a wide-brimmed sombrero with a decorated snakeskin band. The cravat around his neck was polka-dotted and made of silk. His leather vest was decorated with fringes and silver dollars over a red and white checked shirt. Hide pants were tucked into high-heeled riding boots with *pesos* sewn down the seams.

Goldie Santono had been grinning his devilish grin and was somewhat peeved to realize that his gold tooth didn't shine at all in the tintype. But it was a pretty good photograph anyway considering that the art was still in its infancy and some of the more primitive races in the south-west still thought of it as a devil's thing.

The portrait had been reproduced in newspapers as far away as New York and had featured in 'Wanted' notices in various parts of Santono's wide bailiwick. He was no myth. He was at great pains — and that was the operative word — to continue to propagate his own fearsome image.

And this was the man who had power of life and death over young Andy Lugo as he led them, halted them finally in a grove of trees looking out at the area that used to be called Horsemen's Dip, the long tumbledown shack in the foreground, the ruins of the settlement beyond it . . .

5

SANTONO proved to be a good general. There were rumours that he had ridden with Quantrill and his murderous bunch at the end of the Civil War. This was an arguable point though, as that leader had not looked favourably on folks who were not of his own kind.

But now Goldie Santono operated like Quantrill might have done under similar circumstances

He pointed. "Yuh-all see that bunch o' rocks over there to the left a bit? They're roughly between here an' the long shack. Loman an' Bucko, I want you to ride your horses slowly across to there. I guess you'll be outa range till you reach the rocks. Then you dismount an' hunker down quickly. Me an' the boys are gonna make a wide detour and come in on the side o' the settlement, using all the cover we can find. When we are fixed I'll fire one shot an' then you two go in shootin'. We'll get 'em in a bind. Wait a bit though, give us time to get set."

The two boys, an Anglo and an Injun-looking feller with extra-long greasy black hair, nodded their heads. "The rest of you follow me," said Santono, his gold tooth gleaming now as it was caught by sunshine through the trees. "Back a little first, in single file." He led the way.

* * *

Little Cass was at a ragged gap that had once been a window when he saw the two horsemen approaching, their mounts ambling along as if they hadn't a care.

"Riders comin'."

Kellern joined the young tow-headed feller with the juvenile moustache.

"They ain't to know there's anybody here. Just pilgrims I guess."

45

"We oughta take 'em anyway."

"I don't think so. Not unless we have to. Maybe they'll go right on by."

The two men watched. Rollo was now on his feet, but Deegon was still lying down, though he seemed to be rousing. Curly Bess, curled up, evinced no interest. Maybe she was playing possum. However, nobody paid her any attention now.

The two approaching horsemen, still moving at a snail's pace, were not paying much attention either, seemed to be talking desultorily to each other. They were sort of going in a slanting way, approaching a rock outcrop.

"We ought to pop 'em!" cried Little Cass.

"Hold your 'osses," said Kellern.

Then, as Rollo joined them, Little Cass said, "They're getting down behind the rocks." He grabbed for his rifle and Kellern said, "They're probably out of range."

Then it was too late anyway. The men were hidden. And even their

46

mounts were out of sight now.

"Goddammit," said Cass petulantly.

Deegon rose swiftly and joined them, saying nothing.

They heard a single shot which seemed to come from behind them. Involuntarily they all turned, as if they'd had a signal.

There was a fusillade of shots. Bullets tore through the flimsy walls and, unimpeded, through the gaps and holes and ragged slits.

Deegon was the last at the gap where the other three men had been standing and now he shouted, "Them two — they're comin' as well."

Horses and men from behind the rock outcrop, the former galloping like mad now and, as they got nearer, the riders raising their handguns. Deegon got down as low as he could but the cover was flimsy, much of it just rotting wood. He was alone here. His friends were suddenly on the other side of the shack. The attack from the settlement, where the cover was better for the attackers, was a violent one. Where there had been a waiting quiet moments before, now there was the hideous chatter of gunfire and the smell of cordite was becoming strong.

Curly Bess was awake. She lay flat on her stomach and, although away from the not too great protection of the crumbling walls, she was maybe now safer than her captors.

Rollo staggered backwards from his position, one of his eyes gushing blood where a slug had torn through it. He hit the ground hard and was horrifyingly dead at the feet of his friend Kellern.

Kellern and Little Cass threw themselves flat, eating dust.

They propped themselves on their elbows and used their rifles. But suddenly, on that side, there was nothing to shoot at. Men had been horsed; now they had taken cover and there was more of it out there than inside the shack.

Deegon couldn't help his two Anglo pards. He was being pressed himself, and his peril was coming nearer. The two riders were flat on their saddles, riding like Indians, their weapons poking out from behind their horses' necks as they poured a blistering fire at the shack.

These were no innocent pilgrims. These boys were professionals who knew what they were doing. But Deegon also knew a thing or three. He used his Winchester and he used it well, bringing a horse down, its rider flying from the saddle, both man and beast lying still. But Deegon had shown too much of himself and the fallen rider's pard was nearer, triggering his handgun.

Deegon was slammed away from the window by a bullet going right through his shoulder and spending itself in the dust and gunsmoke behind.

Deegon sat on his butt, fighting the cloud of pain, smoke-filled it seemed, as was the shack, trying to envelop him. He couldn't use his rifle any more. He clutched at his left shoulder, trying to staunch the blood. But the next bullet could be in his brain if he didn't manage to right himself somehow.

He let the shoulder go and, with his right hand, managed to get his handgun out of its holster. He raised it.

A maddened horse seemed to be coming right at him, eyes rolling, breath snorting. And there was a crashing of timbers — and a wild human face.

A gun blasted in Deegon's eyes, temporarily blinding him. Desperately, instinctively, he triggered his own weapon and the Colt bucked in his hand. There was horseflesh, a man, hooves, feet, terrible pain. Deegon knew he'd been hit again. He thought he'd hit his man also, but he was never to find out for sure. The great pain became a peaceful blackness and he was dead.

The maddened horse smashed through the wall and trampled the slight body beneath its hooves, leaving its rider on the edge of the sward outside. The man's Indian face was contorted in agony as he fought for life, blood pouring from his chest and, then, ultimately taking his life away.

Behind him, this man's pard, leaving his dead horse behind, was crawling dazedly with blood pouring from his damaged head and into his eyes. His groping fingers found the Colt which he'd dropped in the grass and the feel of the warm butt comforted him as he passed out once more.

He didn't know that his pard was dead. He didn't know that a maddened stallion was creating havoc in the shattered, beleaguered shack. He didn't know that a small figure had run past him, seeking shelter at the rocks which he and his dead pard had recently quitted. He didn't know that, inside the shack, a young whore had crawled against a wall to escape the hooves of the running horse as the beast galloped across the shack where a man crouched beside the body of an old friend . . .

Rollo was dead; Deegon was dead;

Little Cass couldn't be seen any more. Kellern was still alive, still comparatively unscathed — until the danger came at him from an unexpected source, an unexpected weapon. *Weapons*. Terrible weapons now, beating at him. Smashing hooves beating at him, finally breaking his neck so that he died with little more than a sigh.

Soon the place was full of men among the dust and the swirling, dissipating gunsmoke, the smell of cordite and blood. A maddened horse was galloping on into the ghost-town behind, and they let him go. The men who had come in from the town were all in one piece, except for one who sat down now and tied his bandanna round a flesh wound in his leg.

They ranged. They counted heads. Bucko was dead on the other side of the shack. Bucko's Anglo friend, Loman, had come to his senses and was crawling towards the shack on all fours. He looked as if he was wearing a red mask but instinct gave him direction.

"Here's a sack," said a man.

It was bloodstained. But it was full of money.

6

LITTLE Cass left the concealment of the rock outcrop and, scuttling like a spavined beetle, ran for the grove of trees. He knew that the two horsemen who had attacked the long shack from this side had come out of these trees, had momentarily hunkered down among the rocks before riding out at top speed with guns blazing.

One of these men was wounded, had crawled towards the shack and was now somehow out of Cass's view. The other, it seemed, had reached there too, but Cass didn't know whether he was dead or alive.

Cass had seen other movement at the shack of course, but not much from this side. He'd gotten out while he'd figured he still had a chance and so far the reckless ploy had paid off.

He could only hope that the attacking force that had besieged the shack with such murderous surprise didn't make their way back to this grove of trees into which he sank down now, panting like his chest was about to break open.

There was no more cover ahead of him. If the attackers came back here he was a sitting duck.

Or maybe after all he'd be a lucky, *escaping* one!

He looked out. Figures flitted backwards and forwards in the shadows in the long, ruined shack like so many ghosts.

★ ★ ★

Andy Lugo hadn't taken any part in the raid. It had been ascertained that Kellern and his boys had put their horses in a small, almost roofless disused barn adjacent to the long shack. Although the beasts had been startled by the shooting and had kicked-up, not one of them had managed to get out. So

Andy was left to watch the horses. He was unarmed, crippled, harmless. He kept an eye on the Santono mounts also, keeping them behind him and away from the others. And the border gang went on to finish their grisly task.

The firing died. One of the men came out and told Andy that Goldie wanted to see him. With trepidation, the boy limped to the ruined building and entered it.

He stopped dead. A blue haze was filtering away through the gaps in the roof and the ruined walls. There was still the smell of gunsmoke, and a sweeter, sickly smell which made Andy want to gag. But he stifled this, knowing he must not show any weakness before these men.

This was a scene of carnage though, and he'd never seen anything like it before.

As he gazed about him in fascination and horror a voice called his name and his attention was drawn to a small figure seated in a crouch against a bloodstained wall.

"Bess," he exclaimed and he went over to her.

She seemed to be unharmed, but her dark liquid eyes were full of terror and her curly hair was in disarray. She held out her arms to him like a troubled child and he managed to lift her to her feet.

Behind him, the voice of Goldie Santono spoke up. "C'mon, let's get going."

"How about the girl?" said another voice.

"We'll take her with us. You'll look after her, won't you, Andy?"

"I'll look after her." His arm round her, the limping boy helped the girl forward.

A man sniggered, said, "Now ain't that purty?"

Santono halted, as if another thought had suddenly struck him. He was mercurial, hot-tempered, calculating, murderous, completely unpredictable; *frightening*. He turned on Andy, said,

"I wanted you to look at all these," indicating the bodies sprawled and twisted in grotesque and bloody death.

Andy left Bess standing, obviously holding herself up by will-power. He forced himself to look at the corpses, each one looking back at him as if accusing him with their wide and glassy eyes.

Little Cass, he thought. He couldn't see Little Cass.

He did not tell Goldie that Little Cass was missing.

Taking the spare horses along with their own, the bunch rode out, Bess on the saddle in front of Andy. They didn't pause at the little grove of trees which had sheltered them before, passed them by a good margin in fact.

Little Cass watched them go, then he made his way back to the long shack but didn't pause there for long. There was nothing for him there. His saddle-pards were all dead. He didn't weep for them.

He found no weapon. He needed

a weapon and a horse. Those boys had been professionals all right. They had taken everything. Oh, he knew them! He'd watched them ride out, had recognized their leader. Goldie Santono. And with him and the rest had been that limping son-of-a-bitch Andy, and the girl called Curly Bess whom Cass had once visited briefly, though Kellern hadn't known that. Cass couldn't figure why the girl had been taken rather than left a corpse with the rest.

A hostage? The thought made him smile sardonically. Kellern had taken her for a hostage. A playmate for the boys . . .

As for Andy, his treachery had been very evident and completely unforgivable. I'm gonna kill the little bastard, Cass vowed, sooner or later I'm gonna kill him dead.

Cautiously, he made his way into the ghost-town, the quietness and the settled dust, the shadows hidden from the red sun.

* * *

Gabe was the elder of the two by a couple of years or so, being over seventy. Even so, his friend Dicken, being mighty tall and bent with it, oftimes looked older, him and his woolly, snow-white hair atop his swarthy wrinkled face. Sometimes they argued about their respective ages and their lives before they met; mostly they rubbed along pretty well.

Gabe had already been prospecting for a while in this territory — in the hills in the distance that is — when Dicken turned up, a sick man on a worn-out burro.

Gabe had nursed Dicken back to health, but the burro had had to be shot. There had been an epidemic of some kind of fever in a town miles away which Dicken and the beast had passed through on their travels. Hard-up as he was, the man had had to rest in a cheap, dirty dosshouse and had picked up the pestilence there.

He had done many things, but prospecting wasn't one of them. He'd been willing to try it though, and Gabe had been glad of his help and companionship. They didn't find much. They were congenial dreamers, passing the autumn of their years in peace. In recent times they hadn't even visited the hills as much as they used to.

They had spent their dust from time to time in the town that Dicken knew, the one where he had picked up the fever, but which was clean now and flourishing. Nobody had ever bothered them much. Until that fateful day . . .

A bloody battle raged on their doorstep and they wished they were in the safety of the hills. But it was too late. And they just lay low until it had all finished. They waited. And Gabe peered from a window, the only one with glass in it in the whole of the ruined settlement.

"I can't hear a sound now," he said.

"I think it's all over. I think they must be gone."

"I don't think they all can be gone, if you see what I mean, ol' pardner," said Dicken soberly. "We'll have to find out about that. Could even be that somebody might need our help. I think you an' me have had a narrow escape."

"I think you're right," agreed Gabe. "I think we should watch our steps an' all."

Dicken joined him at the window, craned his long length, his neck. Then he said, "Jumpin' cats!"

"Yeh, I thought I saw somep'n just," said Gabe.

"Yes, there is. There he is again. It's a feller."

"Get back outa sight then. You're big enough to be spotted begod." Gabe backed off and Dicken followed his example.

They both got their long guns, Dicken his Sharps, Gabe his old Henry. They went out of their door side by side and confronted the newcomer, a small inoffensive-looking younker.

Little Cass raised both his hands high in the air. "I come in peace," he said.

7

MARSHAL JAY LESSITER was on the trail again, and this time he was alone. He could track better on his own. At least that was what he told himself. He was *driven*: this is what I do best, he thought: I've been a townie with a badge too long.

He had a whole lot more information now which he hoped would help him on his quest, bring an end to the bitter lust for justice which was driving him, as, he admitted now, it always had. Maybe that was what had driven him to be a lawman in the first place.

But this was a bad one; *a bad thing*. A very bad one.

He had talked to Pecos Lil and Madame Drusilla and other frails at the Dally House. He knew about Goldie Santono and young Andy. He figured

64

he knew what Santono wanted. The boodle. And Andy could maybe lead him to that.

If he had to, Santono would start a war in order to grab those rich pickings. And Jay Lessiter, who knew the borderlands as well as he knew the backyard of his own jailhouse, figured he knew where Santono might be at. And the signs were that the other bunch, the express office robbers and killers, had gone that way beforehand.

But surely that bunch wouldn't have known about Santono and his border hellions beforehand . . .

The two forces could be pitted against each other. And Lessiter wanted to be in at the death. He was willing to ride to the ends of the earth — to the end of the borderlands and further anyway — and pick up trail, and ask questions, more questions, and cajole and bully, and threaten if needs be, in order to accomplish what he bitterly needed to do.

"Me an' my pards were troubleshooters," said Little Cass. "We took a job transporting some bullion from a bank to an address down on the border. Somebody must've got wind o' this. Or somebody talked an' planned an' we were doublecrossed. That murderous bunch came at us out of nowhere an' all my pards are dead. All of 'em. And that bunch got the money an' I reckon they figure I'm dead too. They've gone on their way. Godamighty, gents, I'm lucky to be alive, ain't I?"

"You sure are, son," said old Gabe. "An' we couldn't do anything. There were too many of 'em an' we didn't know what was goin' on, just heard the shootin' is all."

"Of course you couldn't do anything," agreed Little Cass. "Hell, they'd've killed you too, an' mebbe they'd have got me as well. I dunno what I would've done if I hadn't run into you two gents. I got no hoss, got no weapons."

66

The other old man, white haired, taller than his companion and with an almost Indian look to his set jib hadn't said anything yet. But, when Cass looked straight at him guilelessly, he spoke up.

"We ought to go take a look at your folks. Maybe they ain't all dead."

"Sure," said Cass. "Sure."

He had to play along with these two old mossyhorns. He wasn't too sure about this second 'un either, could be a goddamn smarty. Maybe they had horses. All Cass had spotted were two old burros. And what good was a burro to a rider like him? And he had to get weapons also. He'd spotted a rifle in a corner too far away for him to make a dive for it — and that might be a sort of premature action anyway.

"Let's go," said Cass.

The shorter of the two oldsters went over to the corner and picked up the rifle that Cass had noticed. So that was one idea gone to Hades! The tall oldster went into a back room and could be heard rummaging in there. When he returned he had a rifle in the crook of his arm; and tucked into his belt already was what looked like a long-barrelled Remington pistol.

Goddamn old fox, thought Cass. He knew weapons, had cut his pearly teeth on 'em you might say. Longlegs' pard's rifle was a Henry, not an up-to-date one, of course, but looking as if it had been tended regularly with loving care. And Longlegs' own gun was a Sharps, a long gun with a mighty long range and a kick like a mule with prickly pear in its ass. Only a gink who knew how to use a Sharps toted one as lovingly as that old bastard did now. And both of them were following the unarmed Cass as if he was Momma milk-cow in a sandstorm.

He didn't want to go back to the gory scene in the long, ruined, bloodstained shack. He didn't believe that anybody was left alive. But, with these two old goats sort of pushing him, he had to go along and, as they got nearer to their destination, he hastened his steps as if in anxiety and hope.

The smaller of the two old men was visibly moved by the sight that met their eyes when the trio entered the broken building. There was no smell of cordite now and no smoke lingered beneath the broken eaves. But the sickly smell of bloody death had gotten stronger.

The taller, white-haired old-timer, still cradling his Sharps, moved slowly among the corpses as if this grisly examination was all in a day's work to him. His dark face was inscrutable. Little Cass didn't join him, stayed near the other old-timer near the gap where they had entered and where the air was not quite so polluted. He began to get fidgety. What if that killing bunch decided to return suddenly? But why would they do that . . . ?

The tall man had finished his task.

He turned back, said, "They're all dead all right."

"We'll have to bury them," said his partner huskily.

"Yes, we will. Then we'll burn this place."

"Yes. I'll go fetch what we need." The man hurried off.

Cass was left with the tall one, with the cradled Sharps and the long-barrelled Remington pistol which looked as comfortable as if it were handsomely holstered.

There was something about this old bastard . . . with his dark pokerface under his white brush, and his sloe eyes which gave nothing away.

"They're your people," the man said. "I guess you should start dragging 'em outside."

"Sure," said Cass. "Sure." And he was glad to do it. To start to do what was to be done and get away from here as soon as humanly possible.

With his fingers he closed dead eyes. But he could do nothing with the grimaces of contorted faces. His old chief, Kellern, grinned at him mockingly.

Well, Kellern had always behaved as if what he figured was the only figuring, the be-all an' end-all of everything . . . So what now, fancypants know-all? Cass was glad to get Kellern outside though, roll him over, hide his face.

The tall man watched, hardly moved. The other one returned with digging implements and a large can of coal-oil. "I guess there's still plenty of dry wood here," he said. He seemed to have regained his composure.

They dug quickly, unspeaking, panting. The two old men were better at it than Cass who sweated profusely. Goddamn stupid old prospectors! They were rolling the corpse of Deegon into the grave when the tall man said, "I know him. He'd be more likely to steal money than transport it for other folk."

"Yeh," said Cass quickly. "Yeh, I heard he was once on the owlhoot.

But I was tol' too that he'd turned over a new leaf."

"Deegon," said the tall man, as if thinking aloud.

"Yeh, that's what he called hisself," said Cass.

"Yeh, Deegon," mused the other. But, if he was trying to prove a point, he didn't labour it.

A communal burial, and the bodies covered neatly. And then coal oil splashed around the edges of the shattered building. There were oily rags too and the tall man struck a lucifer on his thumbnail while his friend stuffed an old pipe with baccy and lit up. They backed. The flames burst, gushed upwards.

★ ★ ★

Marshal Lessiter figured that maybe the express-office robbers and killers weren't known in the borderlands, hadn't pulled anything in this territory before. But Goldie Santono and his border scum were a different kettle of stinking fish altogether.

Goldie was a highly recognizable character and show-off who seemed to actually welcome publicity. He had been spotted. Lessiter had word of him.

One informant in particular had been resting with his horse while the sun was at its zenith and, from the shadowed concealment of a grove of trees, had seen the bunch go by. He had recognized Santono and some of the others immediately.

He said they had a girl with them. Just one, he said, a little 'un. Lessiter wondered, what girl? Had Santono caught up with the other bunch already, eliminated them? Could the girl be Curly Bess? He asked the man if the Santono bunch had had a small, pale-faced white feller with them, a weakly-looking younker. The man couldn't tell him that . . .

He was further forward and hadn't seen another living soul and the sun was not so bright. Light was still pretty good though when he saw the column of smoke rising into the sky.

He went cautiously until he could see the source of the smoke as it began to drift away. But then he took a circuit, seeing the ghost-town too, Horsemen's Dip, remembering it, approaching it obliquely. Then he could back in behind the pile of still-smoking ruin.

He saw a shattered barn which, however, hadn't been burned, though the heat of the conflagration had blistered it on one side. Its roof was caved in, but it was shelter of a sort, a hiding.

As its rider approached the place his horse snorted. And the man said, "Quiet, you jackass." But then he, too, could catch the distinctive smell. Horses had been in the barn, and not so long ago either.

He steered his mount inside the structure. It was empty except for litter on the hard-beaten dirt floor. There was plenty of room.

Lessiter dismounted. "Stay here," he said.

The horse made a tiny burbling sound, nothing like a snort this time. These two had been together a long time and they understood each other. "I'll whistle if I need you," the man said, and he quitted the place.

8

GABE was in the kitchen whipping up some grub. Where they lived now had once been a small hotel which had been built strongly and four-square. It was the best building still standing, particularly after Gabe, the first of the two men to arrive, had worked on it, and then was helped on it by Dicken who came by and decided to stay.

They didn't use the upstairs very often and in the hot weather slept on bunks outside on the porch.

Now Dicken, with the stranger, Little Cass, sat in the main room, facing each other on wooden armchairs well padded with faded cushions.

Cass had noted that both the rifles were in the corner furthest away from him. It was Dicken who'd taken them over there and now he was the nearest to them. The tall old-timer seemed to be dozing but, even so, there seemed to be a watchfulness about him, Cass thought. He had told his story and both the old men had seemed to accept it. But Dicken had seen the corpse of that treacherous, murderous little bastard, Deegon . . . How had Dicken known Deegon?

Gabe came back into the room. "I think there's somebody movin' out back," he said. "I thought I saw somep'n."

"Mebbe it was a prairie dog," said Dicken. "I've seen a few. And there was that wild pig . . ."

"Hell, I shot him."

"And that was some shootin', pardner," said Dicken.

"I've still got some of 'im left too," said Gabe. "Ready salted."

Dicken rose. He still had his hand-gun tucked into his belt. He went over to the corner and grabbed the rifles and handed Gabe the Henry. "There have been some mighty funny things happening around here lately," he said. "Let's go take a look anyway."

Cass didn't follow them and neither of them called him.

He heard them in the kitchen and then they became quiet. Either they were lying doggo, watching and waiting, or they had gone outside. Cass went out of the front door and across the porch and down the sagging steps. He was being impulsive and didn't know what he wanted to do. But he figured he'd think of something.

He went to the corner of the building and peeped around it and saw nothing, heard nothing at first.

★ ★ ★

"I'll go take a look," said Gabe softly.

Dicken began, "You ought to . . . "

But Gabe cut him short. "I'm the one who thought he saw somep'n again. Mebbe it was nothin' at all. I'll go."

"All right. I'll go back through to the front an' see if I can spot anything out there."

"We ought to've told that young feller to do that," said Gabe as he went through the kitchen door.

Going in the other direction, Dicken soon learned that the young feller wasn't there any more to be told anything.

In the meantime Gabe had reached the corner of the building and gone along it to the other end.

Little Cass had heard the footsteps and he looked about him impatiently for a weapon. There was a heavy-handled broom leaning against the wall of the house. Cass reached up on to the porch and grabbed the broom and reversed it.

As Gabe came round the corner Cass hit him as hard as he could across the temple with the handle of the broom. Gabe staggered backwards and collapsed, letting go of his rifle. He was dazed, on his knees. But he managed to cry out.

Inside the house Dicken heard the cry and ran out on to the porch.

By this time Cass was hightailing it around another corner and Dicken only caught a glimpse of him, then ran to his friend who was stirring, striving. Dicken helped him up.

"The little bastard certainly fooled us," said Gabe thickly. "He's got my Henry."

* * *

They weren't being pursued, they figured that. They had the boodle and Santono seemed to think they had all the time in the world, and that was all right by his boys.

Some of them had women waiting in the hideout on the edge of the border. But they could always get women, pick 'em up on the way through if Goldie gave the word. They had to have a share-out, but they could wait for that too. Besides, they had a woman along with 'em, and she was a nice little piece.

After a fast gallop, and miles away from the ghost-town where their devilry had had its rein, they took a break in the folds of the hills. Santono put a man on watch. He never took fool chances, always had a look-out — more than one oftimes — when they were on the trail. And they'd been chased by law and vigilantes all over these borderlands and, on the other side, by the *rurales* too.

But Santono had a network of loopholes and hideouts and helpers. He was feared by many, looked up to by others. He was a ghost, a legend, a scourge, a monster, a brigand, a *bandido*; folks feared him, *hated* him, worshipped him in their superstitious souls. A Mexican poet had written some stanzas about him and now the words were chanted in the campfire nights to the sounds of plucked guitars.

He was a many-sided character, was Goldie Santono; and one or another of his boys was finding this out.

In the hills one of them tried to rape Curly Bess and his leader dragged him off the wailing girl and struck him forcibly, a hammer blow that broke his jaw. It was a sure sign that, for the time being, Bess would be Goldie's girl, although he didn't take advantage of that right then, and there was whispered speculation about how the girl would receive him.

She was but a little whore. Still and all, she had repulsed Juanello when he tried it on, and Goldie had backed her, and one of Juanello's friends was trying to do something with the would-be rapist's grotesquely swollen face.

The cripple boy called Andy was comforting the girl and Goldie didn't mess with them. The boy was quiet and did what he was told. When Juanello had approached the girl, the boy had tried to get in between, but two of Juanello's laughing friends had held him, surprised though they were at this weakly thing's spirit.

Goldie had broken things up. After he'd taken care of Juanello he had spoken sharply to Andy and the men who'd held him. Now the girl and her young champion were separated. She was hidden again by her blanket, a small shapeless bundle in the grass, and Andy sat yards away looking at the ground.

Santono gave the word to move again. Juanello, his face swathed in a coloured towel, moaned as he rode, until Santono threatened to shoot him, and was capable of doing just that. Then there was silence except for the soft, rhythmic thud of hooves.

★ ★ ★

Marshal Lessiter had thought he saw movement in the back part of the building which seemed to be in better condition than its neighbours. Warily, he had backed off into the trees nearby.

He watched the two old men. One of them looked sort of familiar to him, the tall one. But Lessiter only had a glimpse of this one before he disappeared again.

But his shorter companion, carrying a rifle, came right out of the place and along the back of it and around the corner and out of the watching man's sight.

Almost immediately afterwards, Lessiter heard what sounded like a scuffle, and a small cry.

Not knowing what the sounds meant, he came out of concealment and went in the opposite direction, planning to skirt the house and try to find out in that way what exactly was going down.

From his side of the building he could look out at what had once been a higgledy-piggledy main street. He saw a small man carrying a rifle scuttle across the street and go around a corner opposite. The feller turned his head briefly and Lessiter saw his face.

A small alarm bell clanked in the depths of the lawman's mind and he remembered a description that had been given to him by Martha Dromwell of the small young man with the pale hair and scrubby moustache who had murdered her husband Pete during the express-office robbery.

Now he moved by instinct, though knowing in the back of his mind that he was acting recklessly. That young killer was in front of him, but Lessiter didn't know what might be behind him as he crossed the street.

But he crossed it anyway, shooting a glance backwards as he did so. He glimpsed the two people at the furthest corner of the building he'd been watching. One of them seemed to be helping the other to his feet. The two oldsters, the tall one, helping his partner to rise, his back to the man crossing the street, his bulk shutting out the smaller man's view.

And then Lessiter was across negotiating the corner where his quarry had disappeared.

Lessiter had left his rifle back in the

ruined barn where his horse waited and now he cursed himself for his stupidity. The long weapon would have slowed him down but he wished he had it now, matching the man he followed, who obviously had slugged the old man back at the end of the house and grabbed his long gun.

Lessiter drew his own hand-gun, kept close to the wall as he moved on.

There was no sign of his quarry now and no sound except the faint soughing of a breeze. There was no sun and no heat. It looked about to become a balmy evening.

This was an alley with buildings each side of it. The remains of the buildings that is, both of them as full of holes as a broken sieve. Ahead there was a pile of what seemed to be rubbish, maybe a privy that had fallen in on itself.

Nothing ahead. Lessiter looked back. Nothing behind him either. What were those two oldsters doing? But Lessiter couldn't worry about that now.

His slight pause, his turning, had

made him, for a split, *split* second, take his eyes of what lay ahead of him. His eyes missed the broken shard of timber which lay partially buried in the hard ground.

He gave a shocked hiss of pain as the jagged end of the timber caught him in the instep, digging through his boot. Although he tried to save himself he staggered forward, then lurched almost to his knees.

His luck was with him now though: the half-tumble, the presence of the inanimate object that had punished him, had also saved his life. The rifle bullet that had been fired at him would surely have bored a hole in his head were not his head in a different place than it had been before.

Lessiter had held on desperately to his gun. He deliberately let himself drop on one knee. He levelled the gun and snapped off a shot at the pile of rubbish at the end of the alley, figuring that the rifleshot couldn't have come from anywhere but from behind there.

His own hastily fired slug must have bored its way through some crack or loophole or soft spot, for now Lessiter heard a cry of pain. He lurched to his feet and ran, half-crouching, gun held in front of him and pointing like an accusing finger.

A figure came upwards from the pile of broken timber and detritus, a figure that seemed to be swaying towards him, the rifle in its hand levelled . . .

The two men must have fired simultaneously, the smaller one four-square but falling further forward and out of his cover as the rifle bucked and spat. And Lessiter was leaning sideways against the wall and fanning the hammer of the gun in the right hand with the inside of his left hand.

There was a scream, rising above the gunfire before it died; there was a hammer blow that propelled Lessiter backwards, but it wasn't he who screamed. And the other man had disappeared behind his bulwark.

Lessiter's gun was no longer in his

hand. He raised that hand to his shoulder as he groped for consciousness and he felt the shredded flesh and the warm blood.

He must have passed out momentarily . . . Gabe and Dicken came up the alley, the latter, with his Sharps rifle sloped, going on and around the rubbish dump, bending, raising, saying, "He's gone. Shot to ribbons." When he came out he was carrying Gabe's old Henry.

"This one's still alive," said Gabe. "Nasty wound in the shoulder though."

When Dicken bent over him the man's eyes were flickering open. "I know him," Dicken said.

The man's eyes opened in awareness. Then recognition flared in them as Dicken said, "Hello, Jay."

"Hello, Emmy," said Jay Lessiter.

Gabe looked accusingly at his partner. "You never tol' me your name was Emmy. Sounds like a woman's name."

"That's why I never told you I guess. Short for Emmanuel. But I started to get called Emmy when I was a kid, fought like a bobcat till the name began to be like a sort o' badge. But that was in the old days . . . C'mon now, shut your damn' mouth an' give me a hand to get my old friend, Jay, back to the place."

9

"WHEN he came to the Dally House he was always Pecos Lil's man," said Curly Bess. "She knew all the tricks that anybody could ever know. She'd do anything."

"She's Drusilla's oldest hand, Lil is," said Andy Lugo. "She knows a lot about everybody and, when she ain't giving of her best," the crippled young man gave a nasty little chuckle, "she can chat a blue streak. I reckon that, as well as enjoying Lil's tricks an' all, Goldie was getting plenty information from her. Is, I mean — hell, I'm talkin' about 'em both as if they're dead. But we wouldn't be in this predicament if they were dead, would we, honey?"

They sat side by side with their backs against a rock. They knew they would, by the following day (unless something intervened) be at the hideout that the boys were volubly looking forward to now, to the split of the boodle, the girls, the carousing.

Santono hadn't bothered the two of them, and none of the others were foolish enough to try anything now, particularly with the girl. So it looked like they were safe for the time being. But what could they hope for?

"Do you want to see Santono dead, Andy?" asked Bess quietly.

"I dunno. I don't know what he wants with me."

"But you've helped him."

"That'll cut no ice with Goldie if he thinks o' somep'n else. He forced me — just like he forced you."

"Maybe he thinks he saved me."

"Yeh." Andy gave his little chuckle again. "Maybe he does."

"Y'know," said Bess, "when he was at the Dally House everybody had to call him Mr Santono. Even Drusilla and Pecos Lil."

"He thinks he's a goddamn Spanish grandee. Pretends he is anyway."

"Maybe he is."

"Hell, gal, have you got a yen for him or somep'n?" Andy demanded.

Bess seemed to give this question serious thought for a mite. Then she said, "I used to wonder why he wanted to be with Lil all the time. I knew who he was and what he was. I knew he had to come secretly because the law wanted him and Marshal Lessiter would be after him if he knew Santono was even near his territory. But I thought Santono was a handsome man — and he always acted like a gentleman around us girls."

"Godamighty," said Andy.

★ ★ ★

She had not imagined it would be so big, so well laid out and clean and comfortable. She had never been in anything called a hideout before but had imagined it to be some hidden place where fugitives lived in squalid conditions — and Andy was to tell her later that this was often the case.

But this hideout was like a settlement. A small town even, although, as it should be under the circumstances, in a hidden place.

Andy had told Curly Bess that the hideout was probably known by folks who'd be scared to tell for fear of terrible reprisals, but that, on the other hand, some of them looked up to Santono as if he were a kind of Robin Hood or something.

Bess had never heard of somebody called Robin Hood. She couldn't read, couldn't even write her own name, particularly the surname which, in fact, she barely remembered. But she had seen Andy reading newspapers — *and even books.*

He told her that some author back East had written a book about Goldie Santono. Bess didn't know whether to believe that or not. Maybe it was just a rumour.

The West was full of rumours, and myth, and legend.

Andy told Bess that once the hideout bunch had held out against a bunch of *bandidos* from over the border, had sent them back over the Big Red scattering corpses behind them . . . But at odd times the bunch pulled out of the hideout and went over the border themselves, particularly if there happened to be a big force of Norte-Americano law coming near.

On one occasion they'd returned to find their homes had been taken over by a bunch of nesters and their families. Some of the nesters, of course, had ended up very dead. And the rest had hightailed pretty damn' *pronto*.

Once a bunch of bounty hunters had been after Santono and those of his men who, like him, had rich prizes on their heads, Santono had caught them and hanged them on trees on the edge of the settlement for all to see.

Ah, yes, this was the country of the folks who came over the river and the Indians who traded with them, and the *mestizos* of all kinds who hated

Anglos and were more than anxious to warn Santono of them, knowing that Senor Goldie would show them genuine appreciation, would stroke their palms with much *pesos* . . . It seemed to Curly Bess that her friend Andy knew a hell of a lot about Santono and his hideout. Andy was a listener, but he was also a talker, a bragger. And that could be the death of him.

★ ★ ★

He had never felt like this before. He had been shot before — more than once, and badly. In a moment of awareness he had thought that this latest wound wasn't a bad one. He slept . . . But then his sleep was broken and he tossed and turned and heard himself talking without understanding the words. It was as if he was fighting death, cursing it, telling it to go back to the hell from whence it came. He had killed men. Should he now pay for that? Was this to be the end?

Was he old and past it and was this damned flea-bite of a wound to be his *coup de grâce*?

He dreamed. He saw himself. And he saw many others. All mixed-up. The faces. And above them all, coming and going, unclear most of the time but greatly recognizable, a beautiful face. The face of Arabella, the girl from back East he'd met in Kansas City when he visited there to hand over a prisoner. She'd been staying with her uncle, a local constable. She was an orphan, gentle, sweet-faced, softly-spoken, a victim of adversity. It was a whirlwind courtship. Oh, yes, he'd always had a way with the ladies! But this was for all time, he had told himself. She came West with him and they got married.

She was gone now, back in Kansas City with their son, hers and his, sixteen years old and finishing his education, which was being paid for by the uncle who had gone on from lawman to politician, a rich man with shady connections. Arabella had gotten some kind of divorce in Kansas City, with the co-operation of 'Uncle' of course. She'd decided that a Wild West lawman's wife wasn't what she wanted to be any more. And who could blame her? He was mouthing the words now — *who could blame her?*

There was no blame, no guilt on either side. But the hurt was like a knife of pain and the nightmares began again, *the real nightmares*.

The faces appeared, like characters in a shifting, smoke-filled dream. The other faces . . . And the names. How well he remembered the names! They marched through his mind, the living and the dead, the succoured and the damned.

It was Tom Smith of Abilene who had taught young Jay Lessiter his trade. Tom — long gone now — the best lawman Lessiter had ever known, remembering how they'd brought Tom home, the body ambushed, bullet-torn. He hadn't liked Tom's successor, Bill

Hickok, had thought him a wild man, a show-off, hadn't been at all surprised on learning that Hickok had joined Bill Cody's 'circus' for a while. But that hadn't lasted and Hickok, too, was gone now. And so he'd heard was the Doc, but nobody seemed to know what had happened to Kate Fisher ... But, as far as he knew, Jane, whose name had been linked with Hickok's, was still going strong. All mixed up; he'd known so many, briefly, or for a longer *knowing* time, a time to like, or a time for regret and for a moving-on, always a moving-on, a lone man with a ready gun.

The names. The well-known ones and the ones not so well-known. The corrupt and the just and the also-rans. The bad and the good. The Masterson brothers, the Earp clan, Bill Tilghman, Ben Thompson, Doc Holliday, Big Nose Kate, Billy Brady. Back and forth through the years. He'd met Billy the Kid, to him a no-account younker. He'd known Pat Garrett and sort of liked him at first. The law and the anti-law. The two sides of a blanket. Yeh, often the same blanket. Lawmen, gamblers, road-agents, bounty hunters, killers, whores. Sam Bass, Marthe Cannary, J. W. Hardin, Brekenridge, Poe, Stoudenmire, *Emmy Dicken* . . .

Remembering the bodies. Bullet-torn, mutilated, garrotted, knifed, scalped, disembowelled, torn by shot-gun blast . . . The West and its polyglot, venal peoples. *His West; his people*. And who was to blame them for what they were or what they had been?

Backwards and forwards through the years. The young ones . . . the older ones . . . Those who had gone . . . And Arabella, always Arabella. And the boy, the son they called Christopher.

A long nightmare . . . Blood-smoke . . . He opened his eyes and at first couldn't see anything, then a voice said, "Hell, Jay, you were talkin' a blue streak. The most Godawful sound. But not a lot of words."

And he turned his head slowly and his vision cleared and he was looking at a familiar face. And that white hair!

A name from the dream . . .

"Emmy," he said.

"Yeh, it's me, old friend. You've had an almighty fever. For a while we thought you weren't goin' to pull out of it. But like I said to my pard Gabe here, an old buff'ler like you is still too young to die."

"Speak for yourself, pizen," Lessiter chuckled and his shoulder stabbed at him. But then he said, "Me, die from a goddamn flea-bite?"

"That was goin' bad, son, that shoulder. That can happen sometimes. Gabe had to cut it some, but it's clean now and it'll heal in time. How it'll be then though . . . "

Emmy Dicken stopped talking, shrugged, spread his hands.

Lessiter looked at Gabe, a smaller old-timer with a whimsical expression on his wrinkled face. "Thank you, my friend," Lessiter said.

"You ain't outa the deep woods yet, son, and you've got to rest. You've got to have plenty of rest."

10

IT was on the following day that Jay Lessiter saw the medicine wagon. And he thought he was dreaming again.

And on that same day, back in the hidden valley on the edge of the border, Goldie Santono took Curly Bess by the hand and led her to his shack, watched by the brooding eyes of Bess's uninvited companion, Andy Lugo — until the door closed behind them and somebody said something in a low voice and somebody else guffawed loudly and another man giggled like a woman.

But the other women: they watched and they were silent.

* * *

It was a long prairie schooner of the kind that had stood the test of time on many a rough trail. Lessiter could visualize it — now he knew for sure it was real — as part of a winding caterpillar of similar vehicles, like slowly moving edifices, like a line of ships on earth which had given such a conveyance its nickname.

He could visualize it being attacked by Indians and the wagon-boss giving orders for a circle to be made, thus partially protecting the women and children from the depredations of the savages. But many of the women had been taught to shoot and they joined their men behind the wagon wheels or sought other shelter around the perimeter of the quickly arranged ring fortress and loaded and reloaded and poured fire at the attacking force using long guns like Springfields, Sharps, Henrys, Winchesters, the great new repeaters; but even battered double-barrelled shot-guns as well and a few old muzzle-loaders too; and hand-guns like Remingtons and Colts, and Smith and Wessons, and Adams and Starrs and fancy pistols they had toted along. There had been massacres and there had been Indian dead. And this wagon as, from his window, Lessiter gazed out on it, could have been part of all of this.

But not another wagon like it or, if there was, not many of 'em. And that was a fact all right, thought Jay Lessiter.

It was, again, like part of his life passing before him, *standing* before him now. Like part of his dream but not of his nightmare. In his boyhood he had seen many of these wagons passing by the smallholding his parents had had in the Pecos River territory. But he didn't think he had seen one as grand as this one before, or one as colourful.

Across the side of it, just below the elegantly trooped canvas top, was a stitched-together banner with words painted in black upon it reading *Professor Hiram Sinclough's Premium Medicines — Potions For All*.

And beneath this were rows of hooks with varicoloured canvas buckets, their contents not revealed but appearing, very colourfully, to be stuffed with mysteries.

Did 'the perfessor' have dancing girls thought Lessiter, such 'perfessers' usually did?

And Lessiter's unspoken question was answered.

First of all though, the man got down from his high seat behind the four handsome horses. Lessiter had seen travellin' wagons that looked like moving junkpiles, with sorry horseflesh to boot. But this tall equipage and its attendant gear and guiders was prime and dandy, a grand sight to behold. And its guardian matched it: a tall man in a black dress suit and a black stovepipe hat. Cadaverous, and with a black, flowing moustache, he looked like a full-time undertaker. But his movements were spry as he eased down and along the side of the canvas to the back.

And from there the first lady began to get down, and he helped her with one hand at her elbow and the other at her bustle, or thereabouts.

She wasn't particularly young, but she was shapely and kind of pretty with dark hair framing her face. She stood on the sod and waited while the professor helped the second lady down and she was younger, pretty too though, and redheaded.

Neither of them were of the *crème de la crème*. But Lessiter hadn't expected them to be, and he wasn't exactly disappointed in what he saw. He was kind of a connoisseur of womankind. There had been many of them. Before Arabella, and after her. He still thought of Arabella as the most beautiful thing he'd ever seen, though he'd met others who came close — and these two weren't half bad.

Gabe and Dicken came out to greet the tall man and the two girls and seemed to know them well. Lessiter lay back in his bed. Propping himself up in order to gawp through the window like an inquisitive turkey had made his wounded shoulder ache like a rotten wisdom tooth. There was no fever now, however, he knew that; and all in all he felt pretty good. It was his left shoulder and that was good, though he wasn't exactly in a root-tootin' shootin' mood.

Looking at the two girls made him feel better still. But he knew he had to pace himself.

Even so, he decided to get out of bed and was doing so when Dicken's voice called, "You decent, bucko?" The dark, sharp, white-haired man must have heard him moving about.

"Yeh. Gimme a minute. I'm comin' out."

He was introduced to the two ladies: Trudy, the older one with the black hair, Arianne the redhead. They curtsied. They shook hands with him, and the little redhead's look in particular was as bold as the nose on a drugstore Indian.

Their mentor was introduced as Simon Klink and he was said to be the uncle of both the women. He had strong hands and a smile like a death's head beneath his weary, wary eyes.

"Your friends told me of your condition, suh," he said, Deep-Southern inflections in his voice. "I would like to look at that shoulder if you will permit me. I have some salve that should speed the healing process and my own famous elixir which will make you feel better all round, you can be sure."

"The Professor's good," said old Gabe with a smile like a mischievous chipmunk.

"Gabe ain't pullin' your string, bucko," affirmed Dicken.

"Neither am I, suh," said Professor Simon Klink.

"Let me ask you somep'n, Perfesser," said Jay Lessiter. "Why, if your name is Klink, have you the inscription made out to one Hiram Sinclough?"

"You have sharp eyes, my friend. And a good memory. Hiram was my late-lamented brother-in-law and the man who started our business. I would feel it was an insult to his memory were I to expunge his name from the wagon. It is a name well known and revered."

"The Professor speaks true, Jay," said Gabe. "He comes to see us from time to time and we knew Hiram too, a fine man. He went to succour victims at a big stampede and got trampled to death hisself by hogwild bulls who'd split off from the rest, killer bulls who mebbe shouldn't have been with the main herd in the first place."

Trudy was beginning to sniffle in a somewhat theatrical manner and the tall, cadaverous man put his arm round her. He hadn't yet taken off his stovepipe hat. Lessiter said, "I'd be pleasured if you'd take a look at my shoulder, Professor." He led the way back into the room which, with its low bunk, he'd been using as his bedroom, and the rest trooped behind.

The professor was carrying his

doctorly-looking black bag which he'd brought in with him and stood on the kitchen table.

Lessiter sat on the edge of the bed and the two women and the two oldsters watched while the professor divested the patient of his white trappings and then, delving into his warbag, brought forth more bandages, a large round cardboard sort of pill-box and a bottle of liquid that looked like thin molasses.

The salve from the round box was soothing, Lessiter had to admit this. And it didn't smell badly either. The professor's long fingers were supple and, though strong, were strangely gentle also. And his bandaging was a work of art. His medicine tasted horrible, however, and Lessiter grimaced and coughed and asked, "Godamighty, what is in that?"

"I will confess to you," the professor said, "that the basic liquid is mainly sarsaparilla."

"I've allus thought of sarsaparilla as

kind of sweet . . . "

"There are other ingredients, my friend, many of them, of Hiram Sinclough's choosing originally, to which I have added my own." The man's face lit up like a Halloween lantern as he began to chuckle, delving in his bag again and bringing forth a glass jar full of round, black and white striped bulls' eyes. "Suck one of these. They are sweet and wholesome."

As Lessiter stuck one of the sweets in his mouth and sucked there was merriment, and the darker things were forgotten for a while.

11

CURLY BESS was amazed by her first sight of the interior of Goldie Santono's shack. It was smarter than the reception area of the Dally House which was bright as night with the shaded lights but by day looked drab and depressing. There were few visitors there by day, however, so Madam Drusilla hadn't bothered about the decor lately, had only talked about 'a change'. As for the rooms occupied by Drusilla's girls — they, except for the one occupied by the oldest hand and the madam's favourite, Pecos Lil — were mundane and basic, fairly well appointed for their purpose, but no more than that.

Santono's place was obviously full of luxuries and other colourful items that had been stolen over years of raids and robberies on both sides of the border.

Rugs, curtains, elegant furniture, a huge mahogany dining-table and chairs to match — how had this lot been spirited away, Bess wondered? — cabinets full of silver and ornaments and china; in the bedroom a four-poster bed with silk drapes, in the kitchen appurtenances of the like that Bess had never seen before. Though on one storey this wasn't just a shack — nossir — it was a house. It even had a porch — and the whole place was kept tidy by a fat squaw called Momma Inez. She was a good cook too, as Bess soon learned.

She and Goldie sat at opposite ends of the long table laid with a snow-white, lace-edged cloth with silver candlesticks and red candles lit and sparkling. The whole place then seemed to sparkle like a bordello Bess had once visited in Sonora, though she hadn't been taken on there and the owner, a fat oily gent with a glass eye had called her a *peon*.

Now Santono called her Bess and,

along the length of the table, watched her with his dark eyes and flashed his gold tooth at her from time to time. Then, as the dishes were brought out, he described them to her.

After the tangy golden soup — and even he didn't know what was in that — there was chopped fish from a tributary of the big river mixed with onion sauce; beaten eggs, herbs and spices formed a thicker concoction which was ladled over chicken breasts with mixed vegetables on the side: potatoes, greens and tomatoes, with added boiled roots, enumerated by Santono, which Bess had never heard of. But everything was greatly delectable and she tucked in with relish.

There were tortillas on the side because Santono liked tortillas — and Momma Inez's tortillas melted in the mouth: they were flavoured with something very sweet and dripping. There was peach and apple pie to follow and a clear and sparkling wine. And then coffee and a tot of brandy and some sweet, fluffy cookies which were another of Momma Inez's specialities. But nothing more special than the meal as a whole, Bess thought. She had never seen anything like that before, let alone eaten it.

There were small, thin cheroots which, when lit and wispily smoking, gave off a sweet aroma. And Goldie and Bess sat and smoked and sipped their brandy and nibbled at their cookies while Momma Inez returned finally to her kitchen and there was silence.

Later Santono led Bess into the bedroom, to that glorious bed.

She stayed with him.

She was only allowed to see her friend Andy briefly, visiting him as he sat with his back against the warm boulder which he had claimed as his own.

He had found an old ledger somewhere and a stub of pencil and was busily writing but wouldn't show what he had written. She couldn't read anyway, and he wouldn't read his words and sentences to her. They were mysterious to her, almost frightening.

She had seen him write before, back at the Dally House. Letters to folks, he said, and things that came into his head. But she had never seen him put folded paper into an envelope and take it out of the Dally House.

He wasn't as wholeheartedly friendly to her now as he used to be and she guessed he was uneasy about her relationship with Santono, though he'd never been like that about the men she'd had in the Dally House.

He told her that Santono reminded him of somebody he'd read about once in an eastern broadsheet a drummer had left behind in the Dally House. A story about a real-life road agent, one Joaquin Murieta. Thought he could get away with anything, Andy said. Bess had never heard of Joaquin Murieta and she got tired of Andy's tales and his dark looks and went back to Santono.

Santono was much about his business once more. He'd had visitors coming and going, so maybe there was a raid or something in the offing. This place was no 'hole in the wall'. The people lived pretty well but had to replenish their coffers and their supplies from time to time.

Curly Bess was left much on her own. The Indian woman called Momma Inez spoke very little English, only a sort of bastard dialect sprinkled with Spanish words of a mainly profane nature. Bess sensed that the woman didn't like her but kept away from her, becoming more noisy in the kitchen than seemed natural.

Bess was to learn that Momma Inez wasn't the only woman in camp who resented her presence.

She was reluctant to stand by the door of Santono's home for all to see, including the somehow accusing eyes of her friend Andy. He wasn't near her now, there at his rock with his pencil and his dusty ledger. Sometimes he limped around with the ledger under his arm. Nobody paid him much mind.

One morning she was standing by the door, feeling lost, and he was staring at her across the expanse of ground with people walking to and fro, and she was impelled to go and visit him again.

She was a few yards from the door when a woman cannoned into her, deliberately it seemed, a big woman with a wealth of untamed red hair whom Bess had noticed before.

Bess staggered, righted herself. But then the woman pushed her with one hand, saying, "Look where you're going, girlie." She was Anglo and had, like Santono, a Deep South way of speaking, although Santono's way had a false ring to it sometimes.

Bess tried to walk around the woman, but her arm was grabbed and she was swung around as the big woman cried, "I'm talkin' to you, yuh fancy little bitch. Who do you think you are?"

Her methods were basic, her dialogue banal and painfully obvious. She held on to Bess's arm and her grip was strong. Bess turned to face her directly and said, "Let me go."

The woman spat in her face then let her go, but then swung a fist, low, and hit her in the stomach, doubling her up, bending over her, hissing, "I want you away from my man."

So Bess, if she hadn't suspected already, knew what this was all about. And, gasping, but fighting mad now, she straightened herself up and clawed for the woman's face, felt her fingernails bite.

Taken by surprise, the big redheaded camp woman yowled like a cat in a mudhole and staggered backwards, pawing at herself, a thin trickle of blood running down one cheek.

Watchers were gathering. "Go get 'er, Berthe," somebody shouted.

Big Berthe charged at her opponent, who tried to evade the violent rush but didn't quite make it. The two women fell side by side, reaching for each other. Grappling with each other.

Bess, beside herself with fury now,

got on top, used her knee on Big Berthe's stomach, knocking the wind from her with an audible gasp. But then Bess was grabbed by the scruff of her neck from behind and hauled upwards, kicking like a puppy. She was thrown violently and she rolled, catching a glimpse of her new assailant, a big Mexican-looking man with a blue chin and a wide sombrero.

"Get 'er, Pablo," yelled somebody and there was merriment, rough guffawing from male voices, shrill jubilation from female, whose owners were delighted to see this upstart newcomer and new favourite given her come-uppance. But it was short-lived triumph for all of them, including Pablo, Big Berthe's champion.

Berthe herself was about to join her new man in meting out punishment to the outsider when she was knocked to her knees from a slap on the back of the head given to her by Goldie Santono as he charged through the crowd.

Then he was upon Pablo who reached for a long-barrelled pistol tucked in a broad sash around his waist.

He only had the gun partially drawn when Santono hit him with a hard fist at the end of a looping arm, a blow to the side of the jaw which sent Pablo spinning. He lost his balance and fell on his back. Then Santono was on to him, straddling him, clawlike hands reaching down and grasping his throat.

Pablo gripped Santono's wrists and tried to pull the killing claws from around his neck. He heaved and kicked, trying to dislodge Santono who rode him like a bronc-buster on a wildly bucking cayuse. But Santono held him hard now, knees grinding into his ribs each side and the big hands, though being clawed in retaliation, slowly, inexorably tightening.

The crowd had backed away a little. A woman was panting; it could have been Big Berthe. Pablo began to choke, his eyes bulging. The sound became terrible — but then it suddenly died.

Pablo's legs kicked out, then straightened, and his arms flapped out to his side, the half-clawed hands slowly straightening out too, and then becoming still.

Santono clambered away from the body and straightened to his full height. "Bury him," he said.

There were murmurs, but no words. Then men moved forward. The women backed off, whispering. Big Berthe sat on the ground with her head sunk on her knees so that nobody could see her face. Santono turned towards Curly Bess and she could see the killing light in his eyes, the terrible exultation. She turned, moving blindly. And then Andy, limping, was upon her, facing her.

"We've got to get away from here, girl," he said, in a low voice.

"I don't know," she whispered, her voice breaking. "*I don't know!*"

She had to take refuge.

She found herself in Santono's handsome shack once more with the Indian woman watching her darkly from the kitchen door. Did you see that, you bitch, thought Bess; did you see that?

12

"WE'RE comin' with you," said Gabe.

"We shorely are," said his partner, Dicken.

Gabe chuckled. "Time we got out an' about," he said.

"This won't be just out and about," said Marshal Lessiter, out of his bailiwick by countless country miles, not wearing a badge any more. This was a trail of vengeance, of retribution, *his trail*.

"You an' me, Jay, we know the score," said Dicken as if divining his old friend's thoughts. "Besides, I reckon I owe you one for saving my neck in Dodge that one time when Ken Raile was gonna shoot me in the back and you plugged him in the side with that little derringer you used to tote . . . "

"I've still got that," said Lessiter.

125

"It's in my warbag. Anyway, I owed you one before that, as I remember, from that business in Ellsworth when I'd only just gotten outa the bathhouse and was unarmed and Crazy Pete Wilby came at me with a bowie an' you cold-cocked him."

Chuckling, Emmy Dicken said, "Kenny, and Crazy Pete, what a pair. Ken got hanged y'know, by some vigilantes down in the Pecos someplace."

"Do tell."

"Yeh, and Crazy Pete was found beaten nigh to death in an alley in a place called Gopher Creek, can y' believe? He ain't walked about much since then I hear, or tried to pick a fight with anybody."

"They come an' they go."

"They shorely do."

"Oh, f' Pete's sake," put in Gabe. "What is this, home-truth's evenin'? We're comin', both of us."

But it became a sort of council of war, for Professor Simon Klink and his ladies were also present and now Simon put in his two cents' worth and things became mighty interesting and, while Lessiter was trying to figure out how Dicken, buried here in this ghost-town, got to know so damn' much about the outside world, the Professor said, "It was a stolen herd of Goldie Santono and his boys that caused the death of my brother-in-law and great friend, Hiram Sinclough. I owe Santono for that and I've already sworn I'd get him some day, hoping all along an opportunity would present itself. The girls and I couldn't do much on our own, could we?"

"No." It was a chorus almost. And "I can shoot good," Simon went on.

"We can all shoot good," said old Gabe.

"We certainly can," said Trudy, the older one of the two ladies, the black-haired one who had a thing going with Emmy Dicken as Lessiter had learned over the last few days.

Three of the men looked at her. But

one of them, Dicken, said mildly,"I guess you can."

"You know I can, you old jackass," said Trudy. "I can outshoot you any day. With a long gun anyway."

"Trudy does some sharpshooting as part of our sales pitch," Simon Klink explained.

It was redheaded Arianne's time to speak up, and she did so with some fervour. "Hell's bells, I guess I can shoot as good as any o' you. Except Trudy, o' course, she's a wonder."

"Thank you, friend," said Trudy in the bantering way the two girls had with each other. And Arianne looked at her, went on, "I did pinch-hit for you once in the shootin' though, didn't I, when you had that bad place on your trigger finger?"

"That's right," said Trudy, and now they all looked at Lessiter again.

"I'll think on it," he said. "All of it."

The professor had told him in the medicine-man's carefully considered opinion anyway — that he wasn't prime yet, not quite.

Simon said now, "I've got a pretty good idea where that hideout is."

And they left things as they were for a while.

Lessiter still had his arm in a sling as a form of support. But he only had a pad on the shoulder wound itself. Simon's all-purpose salve seemed to have worked well but the 'medicine man', with modesty, had said that Jay had pretty good healing flesh anyway. The ex-marshal had been taking the 'elixir' as well, and pulling faces, but that hadn't seemed to do him any harm.

That evening as usual Trudy and Dicken wandered off on their own. The ghost-town looked almost magical in the moonlight and no doubt the dark handsome woman and Lessiter's old friend had a nook of their own to visit. Gabe and Simon sat in the big room and, from his bed where Simon had sent him, Lessiter could hear them talking.

He dozed. When he awoke there was silence until he heard a rustling sound from behind his door, which was slightly open.

The door opened wider and the girl came in. She was naked in the warm night and the light of the moon seeping through the window limned her in a ghostly light.

"Hello, Jay," she said.

"Hello, Arianne," he replied, easing himself upwards in the bed.

"Easy," she said. "Eas . . . *eee* . . . "

She joined him in the bed; her breasts crushed against him. He put his arm about her and drew the whole length of her against him.

"You all right, Jay?" she whispered.

"I'll manage, honey," he said.

★ ★ ★

Curly Bess was with Santono again. On that day she had seen him kill a man. He had been defending her. But he had done it with such relish!

Yet, on comparing him with other men she had known, Bess had to admit that he was good to her; he did great things for her. Her simple mind wasn't capable of analyzing her thoughts. She didn't understand her own feelings, was all mixed up.

She did wonder though why, after Santono had killed that man, she had returned to his place, to Santono's place. Maybe it was because she had figured it was the only place to go, the only place where she could be safe — and even that thought was a strange, frightening one.

She hadn't felt that she could go to Andy: he couldn't protect her. Besides, his manner towards her had changed lately. Then again, he had said to her that they both ought to get away from here. But how could they do that? Did she want to do that, take the risk? She was still alive, and Santono wasn't beating on her as other men had done.

Was it her fault that Santono had

killed one of his own men? She had a terrible feeling that the rest of the camp did in fact think that it was her fault.

Here, for the moment, she was safe, if subject to the vagaries of that temperamental killer, Goldie Santono who, if she went away from him before he wished her to do so would surely finish her, squash her like a bug.

Men were on watch outside, she knew that. Nobody was allowed to sleep for all the time. But the night was quiet except that, here beside her, Goldie lay on his back and snored. Many a man had lain beside her like this and made noises, and sometimes she had imagined that such a man was her husband and they would be together till one of them passed on . . . And now she drifted off to sleep and dreamed strange dreams.

When she awoke it was still dark and Santono was sitting up against the pillows. He was smoking one of his long, thin, sweet-smelling cheroots and he offered her one and she took it and he lit it for her.

She was drowsy but she pulled herself up in bed and neither of them spoke again for a while.

Then he said, "Where did you come from?"

She gathered her thoughts. She wasn't an inventive girl. But she could lie. She had told men many things, that was part of her business. But she was too scared of Santono to attempt to lie to him.

"I was left in a soddy. I don't even remember where that was. I was only a few weeks old. I learned afterwards that my parents just ran out and weren't seen again. It was thought that Injuns had captured them. I was picked up by a travellin' man who heard me crying. I was starving and sick. He took me to a settlement, a sort of outlaw place . . . "

"Like this one?" said Santono, chuckling.

"I don't think so. A hellhole. I didn't have any schooling. I worked in all

133

ways for all kinds of people and I was beaten by some of them. I was used in other ways. I don't think about those things now. I heard that when I was about thirteen Madam Drusilla bought me from two men who were keeping me. She took me to her place and I've been there ever since. She was good to me, didn't let me go with anybody for a long time. Pecos Lil was pretty good to me too, at first."

"Lil's all right."

"You know her well, don't you?"

"She's my cousin."

"Oh!" said Bess. "But you're high-born. I thought Lil . . ."

Santono gave an explosive burst of laughter. "Mebbe you've been listening to Lil too much." He brushed scattered ash from the bedclothes. "Anyway, I let folks believe what they want to believe. Hell, honey, my pa was a *mestizo*, a mongrel. I don't think he knew for sure what mixture he was. I never knew my ma. But the old man looked after me purty good. He taught me, like he taught himself. He was a lot smarter than folks knew. And he could take care of himself good, and me with him. He died, foolish, had a tree fall on him while he was sheltering under it in a wild norther. He was buried under it an' must've died instantly. I was sixteen an' I was alone. I was a young thief. I killed a man who tried to take me over, make me rob for his profit. Then I was on the run and I joined up with others like me — some of 'em are still with me." He chuckled. "An' we are all grown-up now and famous."

He stubbed out the remains of his smoke in a dish on the bedside table and Bess did the same on her side. The tables were a matched pair in soft-looking golden wood.

They turned to each other. It was as if, with his mind and his movements, this man could make her do anything he wanted. And she didn't mind that now.

But, as he took her, he whispered,

"I've told you my secrets, *chiquita*, but you won't tell anybody else, will you?"

She shook her head vigorously, gasping. "No, I won't. I won't . . . "

13

THEY were ready to go. They were all going: Marshal Lessiter had finally agreed to that. He was no fool, and he certainly might need their help. He joked about his little army. But there was a seriousness about it all.

At first it was thought that the medicine wagon must be left behind in the ghost-town — with the hope that it would still be there if and when they returned. But then it was Lessiter, a good leader, who decided it could be taken along.

It would be a sort of cover, he said, for many of its kind were still trundling around the West. It would be noticed; then *not* noticed. Only in the towns would it be taken seriously — but maybe they would avoid the towns. Outside it might even cause

137

merriment, a wave here and there from passing pilgrims. It could be shelter. It could be cover. It could be left if they wished to leave it someplace. And there were always the extra four horses: Simon Klink wouldn't have wanted to leave those handsome beasts behind anyway.

They got plenty of provisions together before they started on their journey. Not a particularly long one now maybe, but certainly a perilous one.

They had plenty of weapons and ammunition and none of them were actually modest about their prowess with such things, the two girls, Trudy and Arianne arguing all the while. Both had demonstrated their skills back in the ghost-town. Lessiter said Trudy was one of the best rifle-shots he'd ever seen, male or female. But Arianne was more adept with a pistol and nobody could argue that the women were not a match for the men and as professional.

Simon, in particular, was a surprise

to his new friend Lessiter, being sleight-of-hand adept with pistols and knives, though not quite so proficient with a long gun, saying that he'd always liked to see 'the whites of their eyes'. An enigmatic character, the professor, 'a confidence man'; a *confident* man with healing fingers and a healing mind but one who seemed as if he were ready and able to tackle darker things. And, it had to be said now, that there would be darker days ahead.

But when they started out on that morning it was a balmy day and they, phlegmatic Westerners all, did not think of any horrors that might lie ahead, the girls in particular being bright and lively, Arianne shooting warm glances at Lessiter from time to time. He still had his arm in a sling just for support but he was able now to use a rifle — and he'd always been pure lightning with a hand-gun anyway.

He pointed with his free hand, the good right hand and said, "First of all, we'll make for those bluffs ahead."

Everybody agreed with this.

By nightfall they were the other side of the bluffs and they bivouacked, lit a small fire, had hot coffee and beans and a few smokes. Then the two girls and Simon slept in the wagon where they had small, separate corners, and the other three gents rolled in blankets outside in the grass, the towering canvas walls of the prairie schooner protecting them from a small, cool wind.

★ ★ ★

Santono had gone to check on the guards and Bess was alone in bed in the dark night, listening to the breeze sough mournfully outside when Andy slipped into the room like a ghost.

"Get dressed," he hissed. "I've got two horses and stuff out back."

All Bess could think to say was, "Where's Momma Inez?"

"I've been watching her. She's got a man. In that stand of trees on the edge of the camp. We can get out back this way. C'mon, it's our only chance."

Like a living, moving, naked doll, her plump shapely body lit in a series of shadows and curves and protuberances, Bess got out of the bed and began to dress herself quickly, expertly.

Andy handed her a soogan which she donned before he led her out. He wore a similar garment himself and it was way too big for him, but Bess's fit her snugly and she guessed that her young, limping friend, caring for her again as he was now, had stolen it from one of the other women.

He had two horses which she didn't think she'd seen before, but she was far from being a judge of horseflesh anyway. So he was a horsethief as well as everything else. What else was he? He was her real friend, was proving it, after she'd thought she was going to lose him altogether. He was taking his life in his hands. Or saving it maybe, and hers too: the thought hit her now like a bolt of lightning.

Still in a sort of half-asleep daze, she

followed him willingly now, matching her actions to his as he led the horses out of the camp through a route he had evidently chosen beforehand, chosen so that they could avoid the two look-outs.

But it was a perilous trail and they had to go very, very carefully before reaching comparatively level ground and mounting up. But still they rode the horses slowly, Andy picking his ground, Bess guiding her own mount right behind him.

"I have saddle-bags and food and drink," he said. "And I have a rifle and a couple of pistols in case they come after us or we run into trouble."

★ ★ ★

"You got shot up like that before, I heard," said Emmy Dicken. "In the right shoulder I heard, and it was bad and you couldn't use your right gun-hand. I heard you hung up your spurs — and your guns. I guess I

142

didn't rightly believe it though, not all of it."

"It wasn't my right shoulder," Lessiter said. "It was my left, this same one." He pointed to the sling. "It was worse than this wound I guess. But, strangely, it didn't give me so much trouble."

"Yeh, it can happen that way."

"I heard the rumour, y'know? Didn't know who'd started it . . . "

"Hell, who knows how rumour starts? This goddamn country is full o' fairy tales. Legends. Myths. Cowboys are the biggest lying storytellers in Creation."

"I'd killed the man who wounded me," said Lessiter. "Called hisself the Dallas Kid."

"There you go! The Dallas Kid! Whoever started callin' him that? He was a loco cur-dog who needed putting down."

"Anyway. That rumour! I didn't put it about anythin' different myself. What the hell! I was sick of my rep. Sick of young gunnies lookin' for me, tryin' me out, getting hurt. I had to kill that one younker, who wouldn't give, y'know?"

"I know."

"I laid low. I toted a badge in a quiet place. But it suddenly stopped being quiet."

"You told us."

"Yes, I did." Lessiter took his sling down, let it dangle. "This is all right now," he said.

"Don't push it, son," said Professor Simon Klink, breaking his silence in his most avuncular manner.

Lessiter moved the sling back to its original position, said equably, "Yeh, I'll rest it till I need it."

And he'd need it all right, he figured. He was looking forward to that. But he wasn't actually pushing in any way. A little earlier Klink had suggested that they stop at the next settlement, a place that the girls and he knew well and that Lessiter, Gabe and Dicken remembered from way back, though it had only been a mudhole then with a few scruffy folk sharing the territory with coyotes and prairie dogs, snakes and lizards and armadillos.

Simon said that his schooner was not exactly an unknown sight in these parts and they should act naturally, go the usual ways, do the usual routines, sell a few potions and pills and tell a few tall stories. If folks saw them going right on as if making in haste for parts unknown they might start to wonder, to talk.

Of course, it might be better if the three passengers stayed out of sight, watched from the canvas. They had agreed to do this. They had agreed also that the professor could ask quiet questions: he'd certainly be able to get the right answers easier than they would.

The place had certainly grown. But even the professor didn't know whether it had gotten itself a name or not. Folks were already coming out to take a look as the tall colourful wagon rolled towards them. Some of them waved. There were children too, and the tall moustached man in the stovepipe hat said, "I wonder if those kids ever go to school."

The girls showed themselves and the kids were shoved to the back and the men cheered and yippee-ed and clapped.

Simon Klink chose a level piece of greensward and drew the four horses to a halt. The mounts belonging to Gabe, Dicken and Lessiter were hitched to the back, but maybe nobody would take undue notice of them, the marshal's horse and the two tireless burros who hadn't had much to do, their owners spending most of the time in the wagon spouting to the girls.

The three passengers were only able to watch the show surreptitiously in turn from inside the wagon, hear the professor's sonorous spiel, listen to the dancing, the shooting. While the tall man, resplendent in his tall stovepipe hat, sold his bottles (he said the taste of the medicine was a *unique* one!), his round boxes and some stuff in a tube which the others hadn't noticed before.

With her Winchester, black-haired Trudy did some shooting at coloured balls she had made herself with wool weighted with stones, bringing them down one by one from the sunlight air, sometimes shattering the stones. Redheaded Arianne did sleight of hand with her pistol, threatening to shoot her own toes, coming close to that to the oohs and haa-aas and the badinage from the men, the startled squeals of the women and kids.

A bewhiskered old-timer came forward as a volunteer and he danced a jig while Arianne pumped bullets into the ground around his feet. Klink divulged later that the old man, still spry and agile, had been a hoofer on the stages in the mining-camps years ago when they had competitions for everything, including 'fancy dancin'.

Both girls were pretty good with a rope and they did some dancing and jumping themselves to a tune Klink played on a concertina and the whirr of spinning riatas which had fluted paper tied to them to make them sound that way.

Then, finally, Klink moved among the crowd with a cardboard box full of his wares and spoke to folks he knew.

Yes, Goldie Santono and his boys had passed that way but hadn't done any harm. The professor was cautious: this could be one of Goldie's 'friendly' towns . . .

Later Klink said, "I guess they're all back in the hideout now."

Although none of them knew it, in that he was only half-right.

14

SHE remembered Deputy-Marshal Tim Steal, who had been slaughtered in a dark street like a mere cur-dog. He had been her real man, had even said he wanted to marry her. That seemed like a dream now. She had mourned for him, had cried secretly in her grief. But now it was as if that had all been in some sort of other life . . . Before Goldie Santono, who had had no part in that killing . . .

The men who'd done that, Bess had seen them die, had almost died with them. And things had gone away from her; and then there'd been Goldie. And now there was Andy.

Andy Lugo, her old friend. And he would make her forget what had happened in those in-between-times.

"I think we're gonna make it, girl," he said. *"I think we're gonna make it."*

★ ★ ★

The boys had made some sort of stew from an armadillo they had caught. They had 'shelled' him first of course, among much noisy merriment. They'd roasted him first also but had found him tough. Maybe he was a very old armadillo. Nobody knew enough about these primitive-looking creatures, these miniature border 'monsters' to be able to tell whether this one was an old 'un or not. All armadillos, when you saw them, looked kind of ancient.

This one finished up in a stew which had many other ingredients in it and didn't really need the addition of armadillo flesh, chopped or otherwise. Some of the boys said, though, when they were poor they had eaten armadillo treated in various ways and had gotten a liking for it. But they didn't think much of this one, had been spoiled by more exotic tastes when the gold had been shiny, and there to spend on eats, booze and exotic women.

Most of them now were pretty sick of camp-life, so it became a welcome thing when they learned that Goldie's woman and that limping little cuss who was a friend of hers had stolen away in the night. And the irate Santono wanted 'em back . . .

★ ★ ★

Things had been like a nightmare for her, which had lessened into a hazy dream. But now, at long last, she was suddenly awake and following her heart instead of her mixed-up instincts.

And she was following her old friend, Andy, who said that everything would be all right.

She remembered that poor dead, Deputy-Marshal Tim Steal (she could only think of him like that now: he had been part of an earlier dream) had liked Andy. Tim had joshed her about the way the limping boy, who nobody thought was of much account, looked out for her.

Despite his disability — or maybe, strangely, because of it — Andy had exceedingly sharp eyesight and hearing. She was alarmed, her good feeling fleeing from her, as he raised his hand sharply and reined in his horse as he did so. Jerkingly, she halted her own mount. Then Andy dismounted and got down on his knees and leaned his body over and put one ear to the grassy ground.

With apprehension growing in her, Curly Bess watched him.

He looked up and said, "I hear horses. And what sounds like wheels." He rose and looked about him.

His gaze became fixed. He pointed. "We'll be going towards 'em, whoever they are. See that grove of trees ahead? It's the only cover. There's nothing behind us. So we will go ahead to those trees and wait there. It's the only thing we can do."

Bess licked dry lips. "It can't be Santono, can it?"

"Of course it can't. It might just

be harmless pilgrims an' their stock. But we can't take any chances." He remounted, led the way.

★ ★ ★

Santono was being temperamental again, couldn't seem to make up his own mind. Anyway, it had always been a policy to keep people on the jump, and here in the hideout more than he had in any other place, he was able to do this, keeping his people on edge more than ever while they chafed at inactivity.

It seemed that he had been about to lead a party out after the girl called Curly Bess and her friend Andy. Then again, it seemed that he had decided that his leading such a venture was somehow beneath his dignity, despite the sneaky way the two young people had run out on him.

It seemed that he now wanted a small bunch of the boys to go out and find them and finish them and bury them on the spot.

At first he had blamed his fat Indian slavey, Momma Inez, for not spotting the couple running out — stealing horses to boot — and giving the alarm. The woman had told him she must have been asleep, she hadn't heard anything. And Santono had seemed to accept this.

But now, suddenly, he accosted the Indian woman as she crossed the beaten earth in her moccasins, carrying a bucket, making for the narrow, quick-running creek that ran through the camp.

And he had a bee in his bonnet now, demanding, "Tell me the truth, woman. Did they bribe you to let them go?"

He didn't enquire just what they might have used as a bribe. And the squaw said, "I told you, *señor*, I was asleep."

A nearby man, a Mexican called Lecon, spoke up mockingly. "She was on her back all right but she wasn't in her bed. She was on the grass over there in the trees," — he jerked a grimy thumb — "and she was under her man, Bulsy."

Said Bulsy happened also to be near as Lecon spoke. Bulsy by name, and somewhat 'bullsy' by nature, a big nasty-tempered Anglo with an underslung gut.

"Mind your mouth," he said and he hit the Mexican full in the mouth with a fist like a side of beef.

Lecon hit the hard ground with his head and stayed down, while Momma Inez, scared to death now, shrilled denials. But the damage had been done in more ways than one. Santono hit Momma Inez full in the face with a swinging back of his hand. Her empty bucket clattered to the ground and she fell upon it and rolled, her eyes turning, blood running down her chin.

Bulsy's beefy face reddened, seemed as if it would explode. With an inarticulate bellow, he flung himself at his chief.

Santono jumped nimbly backwards,

drew the gun that he always wore in a sash at his slim waist and shot the big man in the leg. Screaming imprecations now, Bulsy pitched forward, his clawed hands reaching for Santono but not making contact. Santono fired again and the bullet took off the big man's ear, serving to drive him backwards also.

"Hold him!"

There were ready hands now and a pair of them belonged to the Mexican Lecon. Men held the bleeding Bulsy down.

"Take 'em over there to the trees where they've been doing their business," ordered Santono. "Give 'em a tree apiece and tie 'em good. I want 'em whipped. I want 'em whipped to the end."

The pitifully screaming squaw and the giant with blood trailing behind him while he struggled and bellowed were dragged to their fatal destination while a man fetched the two bloodstained stockwhips which had served their brutal purpose before on more than a few occasions, only one of Santono's feared rituals.

* * *

"That town where you toted a badge," Dicken said, "what's it called?"

"I thought I'd told you that," Lessiter said.

"Nope."

"It's called Raylondo."

"Kinda fancy. I remember it though. Nice little town."

"Used to be. Till the express office was robbed and my deputy was killed. An' another feller too. An' that cathouse girl was kidnapped."

"I guess. I didn't get all the rights of it. But now Goldie Santono's got the money, eh?"

"Yeh, the real robbers are dead an' under the sod at Horsemen's Dip . . ."

"You got that shoulder an' it turned bad an' for a while you didn't make a lot o' sense."

"I'll fill you in," said Lessiter. "Again."

He did so. And then Dicken asked, "How'd you come to settle in Raylondo in the first place?"

"Do you remember me mentioning the younker I had to kill, was forced into it?"

"Yeh."

"Called himself the Dallas Kid."

"You done told me that once."

"I don't tell you everythin', though."

"No, you never did."

"Godamighty — the names these gunnies pick for themselves. But this one, though he couldn't have been much more'n twenty, was no slouch. He gave me the first bad shoulder. The one we were talkin' about, you an' me, the one before this." Lessiter indicated his white sling, went on: "He braced me in a saloon that wasn't too full. He asked me to step outside. He figured he was better'n me but wanted to find out. I told him I didn't know him, didn't want to fight him. I told him to peddle

158

'is goods someplace else. He called me a yeller dog and threw down on me. Mad! Completely goddamn mad! As if he'd been chewing loco weed or somep'n. But fast, mighty fast. He got me in the shoulder, knocked me back against the bar, though I had my gun out by then. He was fired for the kill, y'know? I could see that. I put a pill in his heart. God, Emmy, I've had 'em easier than that. But this one — it sort of sickened me. It was so unnecessary, so Godawful useless, a life gone for nothing . . .

"I got sort of lost, rode with a sling like I am now. I got to Raylondo. For no particular reason. Jimmy Dallio was marshal there. He'd just been killed a few days before: I got there the day after the funeral."

"I heard Jimmy got killed," said Dicken, "but I didn't know where."

"He was a gunfighter, sure," said Lessiter. "And a good one. He was getting on, stiffening up. He'd gone to Raylondo an' taken the post there for a kind of peace I guess, like me at there afterwards, and you at Horsemen's Dip. Hell, Emmy, I never thought you'd finish up in a ghost-town, playing prospector at that."

"It was a game. An easy game. An excuse I guess. But I was getting kind of fed up with it — and so was Gabe . . . "

"If I hadn't happened along you'd mebbe gone on the owlhoot, huh, you an' Gabe?"

"Mebbe. By the way, how did Jimmy Dallio get to hand in his pail? Did he die with his boots off?"

"No. That's the pity of it. He ran foul of a simpleton, simple as that." And Lessiter was obviously not being funny. "A half-witted young drunk he was about to put in the hoosegow, a simple soul who lived with his widowed ma and was only awkward and quarrelsome when he had the booze in him. He turned on Jimmy and slugged him and Jimmy hit his head on an old ploughshare, split it open: it killed him. The boy ran out, got lost. He was found face down in a creek a mile outa town. 'Twas said he was fond of Jimmy who was good to the boy when the boy was sober. It was said the poor soul might've jumped in the creek."

"What a way for Jimmy Dallio to finish," said Dicken. "But we get it all ways, don't we, son?"

"We surely do, bucko. We surely do."

And what were they riding forward to now, pressing on with the great wagon in the misty, morning sunshine, the lawman who had stepped into a dead friend's shoes and his old friend the gunfighter back on the trail once more?

15

THE lean young man on the piebald horse reached the town of Raylondo in the sunny early morning and hitched his mount at the rail outside the main saloon, although that hostelry was not yet open for business.

The hitching rack was right next to a well-watered trough which the piebald could easily reach with his patchy black and white nose, so he was pleased. His master meandered down Main Street, looking about him as if with friendly interest.

He called himself Ep Swaine but that wasn't his real name, more a sort of bastard hybrid of both his real surname and Christian name. He was born back East and had lived there until about eighteen months ago. He'd been an actor and was good at accents, had picked up the Western way of talking without any trouble at all.

From an old ex-jailbird who had also been a professional killer Ep Swaine had taken lessons in shooting and drawing and using a throwing knife, things at which the old man had been devilishly adept. He had slowed down and stiffened up but was still a good teacher. He said young Ep Swaine was one of the best pupils he'd ever had. Young Ep Swaine was twenty-three or so, and didn't look a day older than that.

He was a pretty ordinary-looking man with a set, unremarkable face and eyes that gave nothing away but lips that smiled to order. He wore ordinary riding clothes and a gun at his hip. His rifle was still in its scabbard back on his horse. It was as if the young stranger already looked upon Raylondo as an honest and friendly town and when a few folks, about their morning business, bade him 'Good morning' he answered readily and with a fleeting smile.

An elderly cuss called Duggan was sweeping the boardwalk outside his general store and he asked the stranger, "Can I help you in any way, son?"

The young man looked at him with a sort of quizzical twist to the lips and asked a question himself. "I hear Mr Jay Lessiter is marshal here. Is he around?"

"The marshal ain't in town right now, son," said Duggan. "But the law office is just down the street a piece, though it needs a new sign. You'll see it though, if you keep a-walkin'. I guess the actin' marshal's in there."

"Thank you, suh," said Swaine, giving a courteous tweak to the brim of his hat, and Duggan watched him go.

A cowboy looking for work? A young lawman likewise? A harmless young cuss who viewed a new town with friendly caution as, in these wild Western days, a sensible man should.

Well, Raylondo was peaceful enough now, and that was a fact.

The acting marshal was also Raylondo's

one and only acting blacksmith and his name was Mike Siddens. He had been one of the last people Marshal Lessiter had spoken to before he left town. And at that time Mike had been in the Dally House in company with Pecos Lil. Mike had left Lessiter with Lil and hadn't known what Lil had told the marshal; but he had a pretty good idea.

Now, with no deputy after the tragic murder of Tim Steal, Mike had been mighty glad to pinch-hit for Lessiter with the help of the old jailer, Saul, who was off the sauce for a while.

Mike had done law-dogging before prior to blacksmithing. He was glad to leave the shop in charge of his prime assistant, young Dick, and take his ease in the law office in the wooden armchair piled with cushions, and him with his feet up on the desk.

The young man who called himself Ep Swaine was Mike's first visitor that morning and Mike was glad to greet him. Compared to this big man's blacksmith's shop, which was like a meeting place, law-badging was a lonesome job.

Ep Swaine explained that his father, knowing that Ep was coming this way, had asked him to call in at Raylondo and pay his respects to Marshal Lessiter. Ep had been sorry to hear that the marshal was out of town. Ep's father had once deputied for Mr Lessiter and, anyway, would be very glad to hear that his old chief was still going strong.

"That he is," said Mike.

"Well, mebbe I can catch up with him. Have you any idea where he's at?

"Nope. Down along the borderlands I guess, a-looking for fugitives."

"I'll stay around town for a while anyway, though that can't be too long. But perhaps the marshal will turn up before I leave."

"Yeh," said Mike who'd taken a liking to the young feller. "I can see you later I guess."

"Take care," said Ep Swaine and he quitted the law office.

He went to the saloon. Being a stranger in these parts, he didn't push himself. But he listened. It didn't take him long to learn what had happened here. There'd been a funeral. Folks were still talking about that. There were miscreants and money to be chased and Marshal Jay Lessiter was doing the chasing and, badge or no badge, he wasn't the sort to give up.

A hunting killer, thought Ep Swaine, and with a wide bailiwick. This didn't make his task any easier; but now he figured he knew which way to go, what questions to ask in the going. And he wasn't the sort to give up easily either.

He didn't see big Mike again but left town while the sun was at its zenith.

★ ★ ★

The two bloodstained and tattered naked bodies sagged in their bonds against the trees and Santono said, "I want everybody to look et 'em and learn. I want two men watching to keep the buzzards away until nightfall. I don't want coyotes an' cats an' dogs an' all the rats to get at 'em, I want that treacherous woman and her goddamn friend taken down an' buried out in the rocks with nothing to mark the place."

This was done.

Then the camp slept while the usual look-outs stood on guard: men had their nights, their turns. Santono played no favourites, even took a turn himself when he felt like it; and woe betide a man who showed up late on watch.

The mess on the edge of the trees was cleaned up and no traces were left at all. Santono even had the two grim trees scraped and washed down. Like a finicky old woman, one man said, but not in the earshot of his leader.

But now it was as if the Indian woman, Momma Inez, and her paramour, big Bulsy, had never existed.

Early in the morning Santono was shouting orders again. He wanted men to go out after that little skunk Andy and that whore called Curly Bess. He had decided not to have them killed on the spot, wanted them brought back here to the hideout: he'd see they got their come-uppance, and then some! He had tasted blood; he wanted more.

He had decided not to go on the hunt himself, acted as if he felt it would demean him to go out riding after such treacherous folk. He sent half a dozen of his boys, told them that too much time had been wasted already. But they weren't to come back until they had that pair with them.

The half-dozen hunters were glad to get out of the camp. The whippings had been a diversion but one soon forgotten. The boys were sick of playing cards and mumble-peg, of bedding the women, beating on them if the fancy came, squabbling among themselves. Chasing a couple of truant kids (and that was all that pair seemed to be) was not any sort of action, and there was no profit in it either. But it was better than nothing.

They left their disgruntled colleagues behind and went on their way. A cadaverous Anglo who had been a schoolteacher before he killed his wayward wife and joined the ranks of Goldie Santono's 'family' was running one of his storytelling sessions, likening the bloody dispatch of Momma Inez and Bulsy to a Roman circus — and he had some lurid tales of his own to tell about such goings-on.

Already the boys were planning a 'circus' for themselves with the girls as willing (or unwilling) participants.

The hunting party was led by a tall, muscular half-breed called Rafael who had a lurid scar down one side of his face gotten in a saloon brawl in San Antonio. This blemish didn't seem to frighten off the ladies (maybe the reverse in fact) and his prowess with them was legendary.

He had once gone with Goldie to

the Dally House in Raylondo and went through all the frails there in one night. He had at that time missed out on Curly Bess who was laid up with the croup. He had planned to rectify this omission after Bess was captured during the Horsemen's Dip massacre, but Goldie had beaten him to it and Rafael, who mightily valued his own skin, avoided a confrontation with his unpredictable chief.

There were rumours that Rafael had a yellow streak someplace — down his ass, one wag said. But Rafael was a cruel, sadistic man and he it was, who, stripped to the waist, his muscles rippling had led the whipping of Bulsy and the Indian woman while Goldie Santono watched in approbation.

16

EP SWAINE had told acting-marshal, big Mike Siddens, a purely-awful bundle of lies. Ep's father, who ran a store back East in a little town called Deepville had never deputied for Jay Lessiter, had never been West in fact, was a peaceful man. His wife and he had been greatly shocked to learn that their sons — and they had another one besides Ep — had turned sort of wild. One of them had disappeared altogether; the other had gone off with an acting troupe and, though he got in touch from time to time, he never stayed put, never came home any more.

The old man had never heard of Marshal Jay Lessiter: the only gunmen he'd known had been in lurid broadsheets and pulp publications, men of myth and legend and highly exaggerated gunsmoke deeds.

Still and all, though the old man wouldn't have known it, of course, his son Ep didn't know Jay Lessiter either, had only had sketchy descriptions of him. But he kept seeking; kept asking. You might say that he had a bone to pick with Mister Lessiter.

It was nightfall when Swaine hit the little settlement of Horsemen's Dip and there were no lights there and no sound. It didn't take the lean young man on the piebald horse long to ascertain that this was a ghost-town, although it was the first he'd ever seen.

He used lucifers till he had none left. But, in the end, he discovered a house that appeared to have been occupied. He dossed down there for the night, his gun at his side, and his rifle within reach also. His horse was in a shed outside. An intelligent beast. His owner thought the cayuse (that was what they called them in these parts, wasn't it?) would whinny if he heard anything approaching. Ep wasn't trailwise but even here had been able to detect that predators had been foraging in this Godforsaken place.

He awoke at the break of dawn, feeling disorientated. The way he used to feel sometimes when he worked as a travelling actor doing the same thing night after night like a performing monkey. At times he had felt he was losing his grip on reality. To his parents, strolling players were the lowest of the low, leading, as they thought, completely dissolute lives.

He had begun to feel that he was indeed wasting his life.

Well, now at least he had a purpose, if a dark one . . .

But now that black cloud of despondency was over him like it used to be and he knew that he had to stir himself quickly.

Even in the half-light he saw that the building he was in had been well looked after, certainly wasn't dirty, was even half-tidy. And the cot he'd slept in had been comfortable, if somewhat redolent of the odour of strong tobacco.

He had only taken off his neckerchief, his pants and his boots, had slept in his long-johns. He was soon fully dressed. He went out back to the piebald stallion who greeted him with a soft whinny.

The ghost-town, grey in the dawn light, began to give the man the willies. He still had some supplies; and he'd filled his two water canteens last night at the pump in the yard, realizing there must be an underground well.

He decided he didn't need any breakfast yet. The horse had breakfasted on hay and clean water and was raring to go. The man mounted up, said, "C'mon, boy, let's get out of here."

He knew he was making for the border, the big river, the territory where Jay Lessiter was most likely to be.

But now the young man who called himself Ep Swaine was beginning to feel that, even if he'd had some kind of trail, he was beginning to lose it.

He bivouacked in the full of the

morning, thinking about the black ashes and charred timber of a large burned building he'd seen outside the ghost-town as he left it. Next to it there had been a large patch of freshly dug earth as of a communal grave. Ghosts lingered in that town, he thought. He'd been glad to get away from it.

The sun was beginning to burgeon. As he hunkered down, his eyes scanned the territory ahead of him and he thought he saw thin wisps of smoke against the sky.

On remounting and pushing ahead, he went warily as he'd learned to do at all times while ranging the West's lonely places. He could ride well, shoot well, talk and act like a Westerner. He *felt* like a Westerner.

He saw the town and the sight didn't repell him. He didn't know till later how lucky he was to have come across this particular town, although he was glad to meet some of the friendly, talkative people as he got himself a good hot meal of *frijoles*, beans and hot cakes in one of the local taverns, with a couple of shots of rye whiskey and mugs of strong sweet coffee he could've floated his hat in.

He was mighty interested to hear that a medicine wagon had passed this way, with dancing girls to boot, run by a tall feller called 'the perfessor'.

A Mexican man said he'd seen some other Anglo fellers also, though they'd stayed in the wagon and he hadn't known how many there were.

"You should lay off the *tequila, amigo*," his friend, another Anglo, said. "It's causing you to see things."

"Pilgrims," said another man, who looked like a drug store Indian. "Havin' themselves a ride. There were three hosses tied to the back of that wagon when it came in. That's apart from the four lead hosses I mean."

"You two," said the knowledgeable Anglo scornfully. "You both need glasses. There was one hoss an' two mules."

"Well, maybe the ol' medicine man sells hossflesh . . . "

Ep left them to their fruitless argument and went on his way. Would he come across the medicine wagon as it trundled along? He rode faster now, though he wasn't sure why. And he peered ahead into the sun, shading his eyes with his cupped hand.

★ ★ ★

Curly Bess and Andy saw the tall prairie schooner in the distance and they agreed that it looked like Professor Simon Klink's set-up which had called at Raylondo on an occasion or two. They had to take a chance anyway: they went ahead.

They were overjoyed to be greeted by the tall man in the stovepipe hat and his assistants, Trudy and Arianne. They were surprised when the two old-timers climbed down from the wagon, to be closely followed by none other than moustached Marshal Jay Lessiter.

The two girls took Bess in hand. The escaping girl wept with fatigue and relief while Andy told their story. The big wagon was halted and the two were fed and bedded down. There seemed little doubt that the unforgiving Goldie Santono would send out a search party after the runaways. It was decided that the folks would wait; Gabe, Dicken and Lessiter stood guard.

In the late afternoon the tall prairie schooner was spotted by scarfaced Rafael and his men. Some of them had seen it before. They'd take a look anyway, said Rafael, the womanizer.

"I thought I saw men outside," said one of the bunch.

"I see no men," said Rafael.

By this time Lessiter and his two companions had gone inside the wagon. The approaching bunch might be just travellers, they thought. But they weren't taking any chances. But then Andy, awakening, recognized the bunch for what they were.

"They might go right on by," he said.

"I reckon that's hardly likely now," said Lessiter.

Bess still slept. But one of the other girls spoke up. "There's only six of 'em. And there's seven of us."

"That's right," said Simon Klink.

"I'm with you there," said Andy, who already had a pistol in his hand. But he looked doubtfully at the tall man and the two girls.

"Don't worry, sonny," said black-haired Trudy caustically. "We can shoot like nobody's business, better'n you ever will."

"She speaks true, son," said old Gabe.

"These canvas sides aren't much cover," said Klink. "I'll try and talk those fellers by." And before anybody could stop him, the tall medicine man was down from the wagon.

"Goddammit," hissed Lessiter. Then he added more loudly, "We'll cover you."

The professor faced the approaching bunch and, as they got closer, raised his hand in the old Indian-Western familiar peace sign.

None of the bunch gave any sign in return, came on, reined in.

"Welcome, pilgrims," said Klink.

"Don't tell me you're all alone, man," said Rafael.

"I am telling you that, suh."

Rafael already had his gun out but hidden by the glove on his saddle, the glove he'd taken from his right hand, figuring he always shot better with bare fingers.

"I don't believe you," he said and that was when, from inside the wagon, Lessiter yelled, "Down, Simon" and the tall, agile man dropped.

A horse belonging to a rider next to Rafael was spooked by the abrupt movements, the shout, and pranced sideways into Rafael's mount. The tall half-breed was thrown sideways, his gun glinting in the sun but not exploding in any way. The bullet from Lessiter's gun, which should have penetrated Rafael's brain, merely took his hat off. But other guns were out now and the wagon folks were appearing, their presence bristling with guns.

17

HORSES milled, making it difficult for the riders to use their shooting irons. It was Rafael, the coward, the leader who turned tail, who broke things, and, in a moment, the bunch were in flight, leaving one of their number supine on the ground, his mount fleeing with the rest, tail bobbing, mane flowing.

But Rafael, panicky, went in a different direction to the rest, going away from the hideout in the far distance instead of towards it.

"That bastard!" cried Lessiter.

He had his hand-gun for close quarter work, had left his rifle in the wagon. He raised the long-barrelled pistol level in his right hand and steadied it with his left. He had already gotten rid of his white sling and his left shoulder was healed, though a mite stiff. He aimed at the tall figure on the fleeing horse.

But there was still activity by restive beasts that were much nearer than those belonging to the fleeing bunch, and the riderless one and the lone one with the killer in his saddle . . . One of Gabe's burros kicked the side of the wagon petulantly, rocking the tall, wheeled edifice.

An end of a wagon-tongue nudged Lessiter in the ankle, jerking him so that, even as he let off the shot, he knew it wasn't straight.

"Missed 'im by a mile," he shouted.

"I think you winged 'im," Dicken said. But, as Rafael had already lost his hat and looked wild in the saddle it was hard to tell. And he was out of range now anyway, and man and horse disappeared in the reddish sun-haze.

"Do you think they'll come back?" said Simon Klink.

"Doubt it," said Lessiter. "Not as they are now anyway." He crossed to the still body in the grass and went down on one knee beside it. The man had been shot in the face and was very dead. Lessiter shrugged his shoulders, shook his head, rose. "We'll bury him," said Simon.

Curly Bess got down from the wagon. "It's all right, girl," said old Gabe, lit pipe back in his ready mouth. Bess joined the other two girls and her friend Andy. They all stood, spread out, staring into the far distance and seeing nothing moving.

Lessiter turned to Bess and Andy who stood side by side. He said, "I want you two to go back to Raylondo."

They didn't argue. They were strained, worn. Anyway, there wasn't much use arguing with the marshal when he'd made up his mind.

They all watched them go, waved to them. The girl fresher now, upright in the saddle, the boy with his ledger (he'd been making more surreptitious notes in it) tucked under his arm.

★ ★ ★

Ep Swaine had been riding in the sun for a long piece, pausing from time to time and raising his hand to shield his eyes as he stared ahead. But he saw nothing of interest, just grass and trees and small hills and here and there bare ground and outcrops of boulders. He paused at a small grove of cottonwoods, debating whether to stop there. But he decided to go ahead till nightfall. An unsettled and lonely land, more so as the dying sun bathed it in a red and hellish light.

Skirting the cottonwoods he heard what he thought was a sudden gust of wind, though he hadn't heard any wind before, might have welcomed it as a break from the steady heat. But then it wasn't wind and he knew it wasn't. The man and horse came violently at him as if from the maw of the redness which played tricks with his eyes, came like something out of a mirage from the bare lands he had been told lay ahead nearer to the border, the big river.

He was thrown from his horse and

then, rolling, the sun not spoiling his sudden vision now, he saw the other horseman, for he had been thrown by the impact also.

The two horses skittered away. Ep lay half-propped on one elbow. The other man, well-built, with a dark scarred face and a threatening expression was up on one knee. His eyes looked sort of mad, and panicky even, as he went for his gun. Ep was in no position for a quick draw. He was shocked, puzzled. But he tried.

He knew that, fast though he was, he wasn't going to make it. The other man's shot was maybe not quite as accurate as he'd intended it to be (this was a killer, and he meant to kill) but it found a mark anyway, the hot slug burning into Ep's side, throwing him on to his back, the agony coming then.

As he tried to pull himself upwards again while his senses threatened to leave him, a shadow shut out the sun. The other man had risen, was standing over him, the red rays glinting on his gun as he levelled it at the man on the ground. He meant to finish the job . . .

But then the tall shadowy figure seemed to turn a little and the gun wavered. There was more of that sudden wind it seemed, and then there was an explosion but it wasn't as near as the first report of the killer's gun had been. Then the shadow was gone, the tall figure was out of sight: Ep heard it fall: the man was down! Was replaced by another figure. There was the glint of another gun but it was held down at the new man's side now. It had done its work.

"You saved my life, sir," said Ep Swaine thickly. "I am greatly indebted to you." He closed his eyes and passed out.

Jay Lessiter looked at the nasty wound, the blood in the grass, and he said aloud, "You ain't outa the woods yet, son. Not by a long sight."

He glanced at the body of the man

he had chased, the one who had led the outlaw bunch and had fled in a different direction to the others. The bullet from Lessiter's six-shooter had hit the man in the side of the head and must have killed him instantly. He lay with his mouth open and his sightless eyes staring into the red sun which was losing its power, bathing the dead, dark, scarred face — not handsome any more, bloodstained and grotesque — with yet now an almost benign, warm light.

Lessiter was glad now that, impulsively, he had come after the man. This yeller dog! He had, young Andy had said, been riding in the opposite direction to where the outlaw hideout lay. But he could detour, Lessiter thought, he could make a loop, engineer a rally of forces (yeller dawg though he was) or steal back on the camp in the night, firing on the prairie schooner which was a good target.

No, he'd felt he had to get the man, try to anyway, not staying away from the wagon too long, giving up if he had to . . . and the rest had gone along with that.

His horse was waiting; and the yellow dog's horse and the handsome piebald stallion belonging to the unconscious young man were tentatively returning. Lessiter called to them in a soothing, beckoning voice.

He thought quickly. He lifted the unconscious man on to the saddle of the piebald and, as best he could then, he wadded the wound with a large clean kerchief from his saddle-bag and strapped it with the wounded man's own belt. The extra gunbelt with its cartridges, holster and revolver would keep its owner's pants up, a good workmanlike outfit of the kind a professional gunfighter would favour; not unlike the gear Lessiter toted himself, though in a more pristine condition as if newly purchased.

With Lessiter in the lead the little cortège set off, the unencumbered mount following docilely, leaving its owner as a corpse in the grass by the stand of cottonwoods, food for the predators.

Lessiter's journey back wasn't long and there was still some light as he reached the medicine wagon where the girls immediately took charge of the patient as he was placed on Simon Klink's bunk. There were, as there should be, plenty of medical supplies. The patient was in good hands. He had lost a lot of blood. But he was still "kinda purty" Arianne said.

"Who is he?" Trudy wanted to know.

"I've no idea," said Lessiter. And he told the story.

Then the professor took over, his long fingers gentle, his eyes bright in the yellow light from the hanging hurricane lantern, for no sun-rays penetrated the canvas now.

The best was done. The tall medico straightened up, brushed his black hair back from his forehead, said, "We shouldn't move."

"We'll stay here," said Lessiter.

"Turn this patch into a kind of fortress if we have to."

Nobody argued with this. They all had fighting spirit, could handle it well and had the armaments with which to back it up. Lessiter wondered, if the young stranger whose life he'd saved had been fit and active now, how would he operate? Good maybe.

But 'the purty man' slept on, slept well, his breathing good. Simon had said that the patient was a very fit, tough and healthy specimen and was going to make it all right. But this was a sort of peculiar position they were all in, and that was a fact.

18

THE four boys were in sight of the hills where the hideout was cunningly ensconced when they began to slow down. Up till then they had ridden at top speed and hadn't been able to talk, hadn't wanted to, had been bewildered by the reception they'd received from the medicine wagon — such an easy target they'd thought at first.

Even they, hard-bitten killers that they were, had been demoralized by the sudden death of one man and the take-off of another, their so-called leader, Rafael. And in the opposite direction to the one they themselves had taken and had followed since.

"Rafael's a yeller skunk," said one of them now.

"He's left us in a pile o' manure at that," said another.

"Goldie told 'im what he was supposed to do," said a third.

"I guess he told us as well," said the fourth man. "We ain't done any o' that. We ain't caught up with that little coyote Andy an' the little whore, an' we've lost Arizona Pete — an' hell knows where Rafael is at now."

"We can't go in like this. Goldie's gonna have our tripes."

"I dunno, he's cuttingly gonna want Rafael's tripes. I figure we've gotta find Rafael, get 'im."

"I dunno." This one was uncertain too. "I don't like the way things have been going lately. Goldie seems to be turnin' into some kind of a crazy wolf."

"He's allus been a *curly* wolf. It's just that he's gettin' crazier I guess."

"I'm thinkin' o' pullin' out, getting away altogether, goin' up-country."

"You won't get your share o' the boodle Goldie took from them folks at Horsemen's Dip."

"All right. To hell with it!"

"You're not gonna run out on us now?"

This was the man's pard speaking and they'd been together a long time.

"All right. This is all down to Rafael. We didn't need to bother that goddamn medicine wagon, could've gone right on by. But Rafael just had to, didn't he? Let's find Rafael an' take him back to Goldie behind his hoss with a rope around his neck."

"Goldie'll have 'im skinned alive."

"No more than he deserves, the back-turnin' coyote . . . But then, after I pick up my *dinero* I'm for pastures new."

"I'll come along with you, *amigo*."

So the two pards were, for the moment, agreed on that.

The other two were not quite so sure. They had been with Santono for quite a while and pickings had been good; prime living in the border towns in-between-times and even in the hideout till things began to drag. Plenty of women and booze and good eats and *dinero*.

The consensus for now, though, was that they find Rafael and take him back. And maybe while doing so get a line on the two fugitives they'd started out after in the first place. Curly Bess and Andy Lugo.

But what if those two were in the tall prairie schooner with the spitting guns? What was the schooner doing in these parts anyway?

Goldie Santono would want to know about that. If they took that news back to him, and the treacherous Rafael in a hemp necktie, maybe things wouldn't be so bad after all.

It was dark when they found Rafael's body and predators had already been at it, had doubtless slunk away in the night when they heard horses approaching. Despite the bloody damage that had been inflicted on the corpse, the tearing and the teeth-marks, it was easy to see that he'd been shot in the head.

There was nobody else around. They

hadn't spotted the medicine wagon again and Rafael's manner of death was a mystery to them. They wrapped the body in a tarp one of them had carried and lashed it with rawhide. Then the bundle was dragged behind one rider's horse. And they all got away from there fast. Out from the shelter of the cottonwoods. But nobody bothered them.

They saw nobody and heard nobody till one of the look-outs challenged them in the hills and, as they shouted their names, stood up and was limned against the starlight and waved his rifle to signal them to come ahead.

★ ★ ★

The young man called Ep Swaine, whose life had been in the balance, was back with the living again. If not actually sitting up he was at least taking notice, spasmodically, of what was going on around him in the now somewhat crowded interior of the

197

medicine wagon.

Because of the serious wound in his side Ep was only able to move his body slightly and with great care. The bullet had gone in deep and Simon Klink had had to gouge for it, taking away much of the torn flesh around it, using an opiate, mixed with raw whisky, to keep the patient supine, if not completely unconscious all the time.

On occasion he had screamed a few times, to the painful dismay of the two girls, though the older one, black-haired Trudy was helping Simon in his ministrations. She was the tougher one. At times, as the stranger fought for life, redheaded Arianne was almost beside herself with anxiety for the 'purty young man'. Simon told her to stay outside with Dicken and Gabe. Lessiter stayed with Trudy and Simon to give what help he could, and this was purely manual, in helping to hold the patient as, half-conscious, he struggled with the pain and the outrage. But the outrage became a quitting thing and at last he was quiet.

When he came to, the wagon was full of sunshine and the canvas flaps were flung back to let in a cooling breeze. Lessiter had gone out to join Dicken and Gabe for a smoke and his place was taken by Arianne, her pretty face, under the glowing wealth of her red-gold hair, alive with relief.

He was introduced to the two girls and the professor and his soft thanks to them were obviously heartfelt. This was when he told them his name. But all the time, though he was impressed by the beauty of the two girls, and the elegance of the man who had doctored him, he looked for another face. And presently the man he sought came into the interior of the wagon again.

"This is the man who saved you, son," Simon Klink said. "Mr Ep Swaine, I would like you to meet Marshal Jay Lessiter."

Recognition seemed to flare in the young man's blue eyes but his features, as had already been noticed, had a pokerlike mould to them. Did he recognize the face, or had he heard the name before?

He could not lift his head high but he held out his hand and said, "I am mighty indebted to you, Marshal."

"You said that before, Mr Swaine," said Lessiter. "When I found you and before you passed out."

"The other man . . . ?"

"He's buzzard bait. Border scum. Waste no thought on him."

Dicken and Gabe came in to pay their respects and the former told Swaine how lucky he was to have run into Lessiter — or vice-versa — then, of all people, Professor Klink and his potions and his healing fingers.

"It's kinda crowded in here," said Dicken and he left, and Gabe followed him.

Lessiter sat in a corner on the big oak chest which contained female dooh-dads. He seemed to be watching the young man. Cynical jasper that he was, he had thought that Ep Swaine's manner on being introduced to the man who'd saved his life, a lawman, had been kind of wary. Gratitude had been there, yes — but Lessiter had thought there was something else also (as if the man thought he knew Lessiter from someplace). But, of course, he had had a glance at his deliverer before he passed out back there on the prairie.

Anyway, Lessiter's watchful eye on the wounded man was curtailed somewhat by Arianne's presence there as she bent over the cot as if she had a young child there who needed watching. This began to make Lessiter eventually feel kind of old and finally he went outside.

Dicken said to him, "Me an' Gabe think we ought to maybe do some scoutin', find another place where the wagon won't be so easily spotted. Right now it sticks up like a busted thumb. I reckon that young feller is well enough now to be rolling, don't you, Jay?"

"I reckon."

"Yeh," said Gabe. "He might look an' talk like a fancypants but I figure that he's a pretty tough *hombre*."

"You go ahead," said Lessiter. "I'll stand watch here. You watch yourselves. An' don't get lost."

Dicken's reply was an obscenity and, with Gabe chuckling, they mounted up, set off.

They were back sooner than Lessiter had expected them to be and Dicken said, "There's a grassy, flat-bottomed draw a mile or so from here Up ahead. On the border side, y'know, it's backed by rocks which will cut off sight of the tall canvas from that side. We reckon the wagon could be pretty well hidden there."

"I'll tell Simon," said Lessiter and he climbed into the wagon.

Not long later the gently swaying prairie schooner began to roll slowly onwards.

19

THE mercurial Santono had had another lightning change of heart — if it could be called that. He was acting as if he thought himself a Pinkerton range detective or something similar.

He wanted to know how come Rafael had gotten himself shot in the head before prowling predators, and the flying variety, did their business on him. The boys who had brought Rafael's corpse back to camp couldn't give Goldie the answer to that question. But they figured that somebody from the medicine wagon — already mentioned to their chief — could've trailed Rafael and put a pill in him.

"If he'd stayed with us 'stead o' running off like a yeller cur-dog things could've bin different," said one of the men. "We owed that wagon-lot plenty. They killed Arizona Pete. An' we couldn't get Pete's body back. That wagon was a goddamn surprise . . . "

"Yeh, who would've thought that a bunch of sharpshooters would be hidin' in a thing like that?"

"We should've gone right by, I guess. That wasn't our business. We wuz after that young cripple coyote Andy an' the girl."

"Rafael said there wuz fancy women in that wagon. An' he wanted to go take a look."

"I know that wagon," said Santono. "Feller named Simon Klink runs it. Calls hisself a perfessor. Usually had two young women with him who're purty wholesome. They do shootin' tricks. But I ain't ever heard of 'em shootin' any humans."

"There were fellers there. I'm sure there was."

"Yeh, had to be."

"We didn't want to go there. It was Rafael's idea. That skunk . . . "

"Bury him," snapped Santono.

And that for the moment was the end of it. Rafael was beginning to stink anyway.

They didn't have a proper funeral and, about that time, Santono was nowhere in sight. But one of his lieutenants, a one-eyed gunslinger called Daiso, shared out the spoils that had been accrued at the killing-time in the place called Horsemen's Dip with the ghost-town like a cluster of grieving broken crosses behind it.

That night two men slipped out of camp with their *dinero*. The two pards who had joined cowardly, womanizing Rafael on his abortive search for Curly Bess and Andy Lugo. They wanted no more part of Santono — who might change his mind and have 'em both shot — and his wildcat schemes.

★ ★ ★

In the draw there was a fine pitch for the wagon backing on to the rocks that Gabe and Dicken had spotted earlier. Here was firmness and protection from whatever might occur, whether elemental or human.

The two oldsters, who seemed to have adopted this place as their bailiwick, were already on look-out on the other side of the rocks, facing out towards distant hills and the border, Goldie Santono's territory.

Ep Swaine was sleeping after the long night and Arianne sat beside him and watched over him. Trudy, Simon and Lessiter sat on the grass warmed by the morning sun outside the wagon and confabbed, wondering what the wounded younker had been doing out alone in these wild parts in the first place. They hadn't yet asked him any questions. Simon had said it wasn't the time, that he was still sick and mighty vulnerable.

The professor was in some ways an inveterate confidence man; but he was a good medic also and had a streak of compassion in him a mile wide.

So now the trio jabbered of

inconsequential things, which was a break from thinking and talking about what might lie ahead of them.

A low whistle startled them. It was a signal that Gabe and Dicken had agreed to give. Like a wild bird whistling danger.

The two men and the girl rose to their feet — and already Lessiter had his gun in his hand. A foursome approached them. The two oldsters shepherding two individuals in riding clothes, guns to their backs. "We caught ourselves a couple pigeons," said Dicken with a grin a mile wide on his dark, hatchet face.

"Two of the bunch who attacked us earlier," said Gabe. "I recognized them."

"I guess you're right," said Lessiter. "Are their horses back there?"

"Yeh."

"I'll go get 'em," said Trudy and hastened away.

"Hang 'em," said Lessiter and he turned and pointed.

The draw was flat and grassy apart from the rock outcrops at one end, and one other thing: a single tree of indeterminate genus which had obviously been the victim of a bolt of lightning during one of the violent flash storms that hit this part of the world from time to time. It was blackened at the trunk and the rest of it bare and twisted with branches off at strange angles. It was a hangman's nightmare, but a practical one if anybody looked at it in a particular way. And Marshal Lessiter was obviously looking at it in just that way.

The eyes of the two captives bugged from their heads and one of them said, "You can't do that."

The other one, who'd regained his composure and looked suddenly as if he wouldn't be scared of the Devil himself, said, "He'll do it if he says he will. That's Jay Lessiter, I've seen the old son-bitch before."

Even Gabe and Dicken had looked startled. And Simon Kling was visibly outraged and momentarily at a loss for words.

* * *

As Curly Bess and Andy climbed the steps to the porch of the Dally House they could hear the shrill tones of Drusilla ringing out. She was obviously favouring somebody with a large piece of her mind.

The somebody proved to be one of her bully-boys whose tail could be seen disappearing through a door as the two young people walked into the now silent lobby. There would be no customers yet awhile.

Drusilla turned in surprise. Then her eyes almost popped from her fleshy but not unhandsome face as she threw up her arms, crying, "Godamighty!"

She wasn't usually given to profanity of any kind and dissuaded her girls from using any such language. But she was beside herself now with a kind of amazement.

"Oh, shit-damn an' trot cakes, I thought you two were dead."

"We've been to hell and we've consorted with the Devil," Andy Lugo said. "But now we're back."

Drusilla caught Bess in a bearlike embrace and the small young girl began to weep.

"Lil," bellowed Drusilla.

A half-dressed Pecos Lil appeared at the top of the stairs and demanded, "What's in hell's got into yuh, Dru? Cain't nobody sleep in this goddam chicken-run?"

Despite the big madam's strictures her oldest 'girl' seldom minced words. But now she came down the stairs as if she been poked in her bustle (non-existent) with a redhot stick, screaming, "Bess. Andy. By all that's holy."

The three people did a sort of little dance in the lobby, not so ornate in daylight, but colourful. And heads appeared and peering eyes and there were exclamations of surprise and delight.

"Come on," said Drusilla. "You two of gotta get cleaned up and seen to, an' I want to know where you've been and what you've done."

"You look after Bess," said Andy. "I haven't got time to stop now but I will look in again later. Who's in the law office now? There's just got to be somebody."

"It's Big Mike Siddens the blacksmith," said Drusilla. She'd seen the limping younker in an obstreperous mood before and didn't bother to argue with him.

"That big cuss ain't been to see me for days," whined Pecos Lil.

"Nor he won't I guess," Andy flung over his shoulder as he made purposefully for the door.

He found the big lawman in the office and was greeted with something akin to merriment. But Mike soon cooled off when he heard what Andy wanted.

The big blacksmith-cum-law officer became stern and officious, buckling on

211

his gunbelt, saying, "I'll get some boys together. I'll leave ol' Saul in charge here — he can cut it."

"I'll go back to the Dally House and get ready. Will you pick me up there?"

"We will . . . What's that you've got under your arm, pardner?"

It was the large tattered ledger. Andy had almost forgotten he still had it, had clung to it, but now more important things were at hand. He said, "Just somep'n I picked up on my travels."

Old Saul, the jailer, came in from the back and, as Andy left the office, he could hear big Mike begin to give out with the orders.

20

DICKEN and Gabe had naturally relieved the two outlaws of their armaments as soon as they captured them. Now, at Lessiter's orders, they searched the two partners more thoroughly and came up with quite a stash of greenbacks and gold coins. While this was going on Professor Klink could be heard quietly but forcefully arguing with Lessiter in the background.

Both men turned as old Gabe said, "Look at this."

Lessiter spoke quickly then, glaring at the two men. "That's part of the loot, isn't it, that you took off the bunch in that fight at Horsemen's Dip?"

"What if it is? They were robbers an' killers. An' what are you? You killed our pard, Arizona Pete."

"You came at us. But I'm not gonna argue with you."

Lessiter turned to Gabe and Dicken, went on, "March 'em over to that tree. Let's finish with this."

"Move," said Dicken.

Gabe didn't say anything.

Simon Klink stood silently in the background. Trudy, who had gone into the wagon and then come out again, stood in equal silence on the collapsable step. This was, strangely, still a peaceful scene.

But things changed dramatically as the most talkative of the two outlaws, the feisty one, suddenly whirled about, swinging at Lessiter. But Dicken was quicker, swinging with his gun, the barrel catching the man with a soft thud on the side of the head.

The man went down as if from a powerful, high-stepping kick. He tried to struggle upwards but then fell on his face.

His partner said shrilly, "You can't do this. You can't do it!"

"Get 'im up," said Lessiter.

The half-conscious man was hauled to his feet by old Gabe who still wasn't saying a word.

The second man put his hands on his partner's shoulder to steady him and help him along.

The cortège of Lessiter, Gabe and Dicken with their two captives reached the bare and grotesque tree while Trudy and Simon gazed after them as if helplessly. And now Arianne came out of the wagon, gesticulating and talking, though the hanging party under the tree couldn't hear her words.

* * *

The second man could be seen wildly protesting while his damaged partner drew himself up as if defiantly. Suddenly old Gabe turned about, come back. "We ain't got a rope," he said.

"That's a mercy," said tall Simon. "I'm not going to give you one."

"I've got some rawhide," said Gabe

and went to one of the burros standing patiently chewing cud. He got a stout-looking riata. He now seemed strangely resigned to what was about to happen.

"You've got to stop them," Klink said.

Gabe didn't answer, passed on, his pipe still in his mouth but obviously unlit.

★ ★ ★

The rope was ready. The three executioners and two condemned prisoners stood beneath the grotesque tree.

The talky outlaw, half-stunned, had been silent, a swelling cut at his temple, blood trickling down his cheek. But he was still the defiant one, and suddenly he spoke up again.

"You're killin' us off, ain't you? You killed Rafael as well I guess."

"Rafael?" echoed Lessiter. "He the tall, dark, scarfaced one who rode off in a different direction to the rest o' yuh?"

"Yeh. A yaller dawg."

"I killed him," said Lessiter. "To save a man he'd already wounded and was aiming to finish." He jerked a thumb. "A young man who's lyin' back there in the wagon right now."

"What you aiming to do then — kill us all off?"

"We're wasting time," said Lessiter. "And you talk too much. Put the rope on him, Gabe."

"You ain't got no hosses," said the man.

"We'll take you one at a time and haul on you," said Lessiter. "You ever seen that done, bucko? It can be mighty slow hanging, I'm tellin' you."

"That Rafael," said the other outlaw in a shaky voice, "he was as crazy as Goldie Santono. That the one you're after; are you after Santono?"

"I'll tell you somep'n now," said the defiant one. "Santono an' his boys'll be too much for you." He had the rope around his neck now but Gabe hadn't yet pulled it tight.

"We wuz gettin' away from there, me an' Ben," said the second outlaw. "We wanted no more of that mob an' that Santono — Crazy . . . " He seemed as if he were about to weep.

"You can't get at that hideout," said the man called Ben. "They'd slaughter you before you . . . " He choked as, at a sign from Lessiter, Gabe jerked on the rope, the man swaying.

"That ain't hard enough," said Gabe's pard, Dicken. "Give me that rawhide."

"We know a back way," shrilled Ben's partner. "I'll take you. We came out that way. I'll show you. If you'll let Ben an' me free I'll show you."

Dicken wasn't as hesitant as Gabe. He was ruthless. Ben choked wordlessly, his wounded face suffusing with blood. Lessiter made a gesture to Dicken, who slackened the rope.

"Your ears ain't stopped, bucko," said Lessiter. "You heard what your pard said, didn't you?"

But some signal must have been

exchanged again: Dicken threw the end of the rope over a convenient twisted bough and yanked. Ben seemed as if he was about to say something; but he choked.

"Didn't you?" repeated Lessiter mercilessly.

Ben managed to nod his head.

"So?"

Ben nodded again — very slowly.

"How about the money?" asked the other outlaw, gaining heart.

"Don't be so goddam cheeky," Lessiter told him. "The money goes back where it belongs. Still an' all, I ain't gonna hang you now, not yet, you'll be glad o' that. I ain't promising anything. I want results. If I get 'em, you get a chance for life. If not, I might shoot you both outa hand anyway."

The cortège returned to the wagon. Dicken said in an aside to Simon Klink, "I told you to wait, didn't I, *amigo*? I know how Jay operates. He's tricky; full of 'em. A bit like yourself I guess."

Simon smiled thinly, nodded wordlessly. The listening Gabe grumbled, "He fooled me for a while anyway."

The co-operative outlaw, watched sullenly by his friend Ben, untalkative now, was telling Lessiter that Goldie Santono already knew of the medicine wagon's presence in the territory and would maybe want to do something about it when the fancy took him. You never knew with Goldie . . .

But it was best not to wait. And they could detour. The man was pointing, gesticulating.

Simon went into the wagon, came out. "We can move now if you want to," he said, as if answering a question.

The two outlaws were put on their horses' backs with their hands tied. "All right, let's move." Lessiter pointed with a long finger. "That way."

"Me an' Gabe will range each side an' scout, Jay," said Dicken.

"Go ahead."

There was still a lot of daylight left, a lot of space and very little cover.

But they were making a wide detour, the hills to the left of them now, still pretty indistinct in the heat-haze so that any vision from that direction would be difficult. They didn't go too fast. They went warily, keeping both Gabe and Dicken in sight most of the time, though losing sight of one or the other of them at intervals, never both at the same time, Lessiter watching with a restless gaze. This was a professional operation now led by a professional hunter and man-killer.

21

SIMON KLINK drove the wagon, with black-haired Trudy on the seat beside him, her rifle across her lap. Lessiter rode behind the two prisoners, keeping an eye on them as well as on the surrounding terrain. Red-haired Arianne was still in the inside of the wagon with Ep Swaine, but she peeped out from time to time, and each time she had a pistol in her hand. Her concern for her 'purty young man' wasn't going to prevent her doing whatever duty might be called for — and Lessiter had seen how dutiful she could be with firearms.

She poked out her red head between the two personages on the wagon seat and remarked that young Ep now seemed to be raring to go, whatever that meant under the circumstances. And it was just after this that Lessiter called a halt in a sparse grove of trees which would give them a little hiding and shelter, signalling Gabe and Dicken to come in before the light got too bad. The sun was sinking below the rim of the hills which were still over to the left of them. The two outlaws — and even Ben was more co-operative now — had said they'd have to 'swing in' soon. The sky was in a red wash like blood slowly running below the hills behind them, to dissipate among the silent, waiting crags.

The night fell suddenly as it often did in these parts. A dark night with a pale slice of moon and few stars, most of which were hidden behind scudding clouds of a dark complexion. Simon Klink said it looked as if they might have some rain, that he'd felt it in his bones a mite earlier.

In the wagon Arianne made a small meal with coffee and brought it out to them as they hunkered in the grass. Lessiter had put the two prisoners apart so they couldn't talk to each other.

They both ate their grub avidly as if they thought it might be their last. Lessiter left them under the watchful eyes of the others and climbed into the wagon. Having finished the food he took the hot coffee in with him.

Ep Swaine was propped up in the cot and Arianne, who had returned to her post, was in an Indian squat beside him.

"Go outside, honey," Lessiter told her. "Lie in the grass awhile and take your ease. Sleep if you can."

"All right." As she quitted them, the two men looked at each other.

"You're going after Goldie Santono and his bunch, aren't you, Jay?" said Swaine. It was the first time he'd called Lessiter by his Christian name instead of addressing him as Marshal. "I've heard of that bunch."

"Who ain't?" said the other man laconically. "But you ain't a Westerner are you, Ep?"

"I didn't fool you, did I?"

"You did for a while. You're good."

"I used to be an actor."

"Do tell. There ain't many openings for that sort of thing in these wide-open spaces. So what brought you here?"

"You're pretty blunt at asking questions, aren't you, Marshal?" said Swaine.

"I'm a lawman. I'm paid to ask questions. I'm way outa my bailiwick now, way outa my jurisdiction. But I'm after some killers an' robbers who have money belonging to my town. I want all of it — and then some!"

"I see your point, Jay," said Swaine, more mildly now.

"Besides," said Lessiter, "I know you've been watching me purty closely since you came back to the land o' the living. Are you on the run?"

"Not so's you'd notice." Swaine used a Westernism now.

"So you just wanted to come from East to West, huh? Or did you have any partic'lar reason for coming West?"

"I guess I did; thought I did."

Dicken, hatless, poked his white head

through the tent-flap, said urgently, "Riders approaching. Think they came outa the hills. But not sure they're comin' in this direction."

Lessiter started forward. Behind him, Ep Swaine said, "Maybe you ought to give me a gun."

"I'll see to it," said Lessiter. Then he was gone.

He had put the young man's own gear under a tarp at Simon Klink's end of the long, partitioned vehicle, wasn't sure just why he'd done that, precautionary instinct maybe. He didn't know whether Swaine knew where the gear was or not. Maybe Arianne had told him. She and her 'purty' man were getting mighty thick.

Hell, you're not getting jealous are you, he asked himself? Then in the same breath, likely, he thought of dark Martha waiting for him back in Raylondo. Martha, his secret lover, whose husband had been murdered by bandits who were themselves lost and buried. A tragic train of events. And was there to be the end of it soon?

A mixed-up mind. But only a temporary lapse. And somebody was shouting now and there was the thud of hasty hooves.

There was a single shot. Gabe stood with a smoking gun in his hand. "That crazy man," he babbled. "I was watching 'em, with their hands untied, eating their grub. He heard them hosses and he jumped, ran. He made it to his own horse . . . "

But he hadn't made it any further, defiant, reckless Ben. The horse had skittered away, was still now, head turned enquiringly. Ben lay supine in the grass nearer to the camp. Dicken was nearest to the body, bent over it.

"Dead as a skunk. Plumb in the back o' the skull. That was good shootin', pardner."

Gabe was visibly shaken. "You had to do it," Dicken told him. "It could've been me who did it."

"Or me," said Trudy who had her gun in her hand.

"You was just quicker, Gabe," said Dicken.

"Listen," said Lessiter, dropping on one knee, inclining his head.

"They're coming this way now I guess," he went on.

"They must've heard the shot," said Gabe. "I should've gone after him, slugged him."

"Maybe they heard his shouting anyway," said Lessiter. "No good arguing about that now."

Arianne's voice was suddenly raised from the wagon. Then her face appeared in the tent-flap and it was pushed aside and Ep Swaine was next to her and she was holding him.

"My weapons," said Swaine. "Make no mistake, I can use them. I'm good."

"I know where you put 'em, Jay," said Arianne.

"Get 'em for him then."

Lessiter turned and pointed at the second captive who didn't seem to have moved, seemed to be staring at the body of his late partner lying face downwards a few yards ahead. "Put him under the wagon. Leave the body where it is, we ain't got time to do much else with it. We want this spot fortified as best we can make it."

"Plenty of cover in the wagon and slits in the sides we can open," said Simon. "Place under the wagon too, round the wheels. I'll unhitch the horses and take them behind that," — the tall man pointed — "put them with the other mounts and the burros."

The camp with the tall prairie schooner in the centre of it was soon a maelstrom of activity but everything being done with more precision than seemed likely. And there were infinitesimal pauses for listening.

And the sound of hooves was getting louder.

The sky had darkened, and suddenly everybody was made aware very dramatically of this fact. Thunder rolled. The sky over the hills which had been red hot not so long ago was split by jagged lightning; and then the rain came.

Slashing, needle-sharp. Cold too. "I told you so," yelled Simon Klink as everybody ran for cover.

Cover from the savage elements as well as the savage humans who bore down on them, though the sound of the hooves was blanketed by the violent clamour of the storm.

In the small clearing surrounded by trees the camp with the prairie schooner in the centre of it was partially sheltered by the driving rain. The attacking party came into the trees fast.

The trees were not closely bunched: this couldn't be called a wood. But now the night was dark and the rain made visibility even worse than it had been before. The attackers' charge became an abortive one and horses swerved and slid and chittered and one rider was caught by a swinging branch disturbed by another horseman who'd gone before him. The caught man hit the ground hard, was narrowly missed by another startled beast. Dazed, the man staggered in the darkness, looking for his mount, seeing nothing now but wild, bewildering shapes.

The attackers were firing. But so were the folks at the wagon. The unmounted outlaw took a slug in the belly and screamed in shock, and then agony as he clutched at himself and collapsed to the ground again, gasping and writhing.

Santono himself was leading the raid. It had figured that they'd come out of the hideout more than a mite too late; but the leader had made up his mind at the last minute as he often did and the boys, chafing at recent inactivity, had been glad to follow him.

Even then they would've missed their quarry if they hadn't heard the shouting voice, followed by the single gunshot. This was when Santono had gone into his great cavalry act, the general leading his troops, turning them with a sweep of his long arm and a yell of command, then galloping away in front of them, the men following like the ragged tail of a wild kite.

The sudden rain and the lightning and thunder were no help at all and they came upon the grove of trees precipitately as they loomed up out of the darkness and then, as they hit them, were lit in a ghostly way by lightning, the jagged forks of which seemed much nearer now, threatening to spook the horses.

The rain seemed to be crashing into the trees as if threatening to destroy them and the lightning and thunder played a devilish game. Visibility was almost nil between the flashes of lightning and the tongues of fire from guns which boomed among the trees. The tall medicine wagon was like a ghost thing seen only fitfully. But it was a big target and the outlaws made the most of that.

They couldn't ride around it Injun-fashion: there wasn't enough space. Blistering fire was coming at them and one man was already down.

The attackers couldn't actually see the defenders at the wagon. Only their gunflashes were a guide. But the defenders seemed pretty well entrenched. The shot that had got one of the outlaws in the belly had come from low down.

Gabe, Dicken and Lessiter were under the wagon, sheltering behind a couple of packing cases filled with various gee-gaws and a long packed oblong of hay which had only been chewed a mite at a corner by one of the burros.

With this trio was the late Ben's pard, lucky to be still alive, though his hands were bound now. He was protected from harm by the men around him, unless a stray bullet had his name on it.

Ep Swaine, Simon Klink and the two girls were in the wagon, well protected by the gear which stood and hung and was jumbled around them. They used slits in the tall trooped canvas and worked on both long sides of the now stationary edifice and poured fire at anything that moved.

They had been able to notice that two still bodies lay out there, in gaps lit fitfully by the lightning. It was a pity that one of the bodies was that of outlaw Ben who'd been killed earlier by Gabe, that temporarily disorientated oldster who was giving a good account of himself now from under the wagon. The defenders had plenty of weapons and ammunition and maybe Goldie Santono hadn't taken full knowledge of that beforehand, though he should've done . . .

Ep, Simon and Trudy all had Winchester repeating rifles. Of the three of them, sharpshooting black-haired Trudy was undeniably the best; but to the surprise of the rest, Ep Swaine was a cracker also and didn't seem to be letting his wounded side bother him too much. Red-haired Arianne had an older type but skilfully modified Remington long gun which seemed to shoot as fast as the Winchesters and, though not so professionally prime as her friend, Trudy, the red-haired girl wasn't half bad, and as cool as cold beer.

The two girls and the wounded young man had a Colt apiece, almost a matching trio. But Simon had an older model of Mr Samuel Colt's now bewildering selection of hand-guns, a heavy long-barrelled Dragoon which bucked in the tall medico's long hand, had a roar like a miniature cannon and filled the interior of the wagon with black smoke.

This was a sort of miniature field of battle — and outside seemed to match it, and exaggerate and intensify it in a hellish way.

Under the wagon Gabe had his old Henry long gun, Dicken his Sharps, both of them lovingly cared for and in pristine condition. They had pistols; Dicken a Remington, Gabe a shorter-barrelled Smith and Wesson.

Lessiter had a Winchester rifle and a Colt .45 and, though it was in the back of his belt and he called it his 'sneak gun', a double-barrelled ('over-and-under') derringer. No good at a long range but lethal at close quarters; dandy if, for instance, Lessiter decided to shoot the roped captive to stop him at his caterwauling. But the man surprised him now, screaming in his ear.

"Give me a gun f' Chrissakes an' let me shoot some o' the bastards. I don't owe 'em anything."

Lessiter handed over his own rifle, said, "Point that right out, bucko, an' shoot straight. Don't turn it this way or I'll put a bullet in your brain."

The man was awkward. "Cut this goddamn rope then."

"Sorry." With his jack-knife Lessiter did that little task and the outlaw said "Thanks" sarcastically, leaned forward, butted the Winchester to his shoulder, rested his cheek upon it.

The firing on both sides now was blistering, a cacophony of terror.

22

THE first bullet that struck Goldie Santono came from a gun levelled from under the prairie schooner. He was hit in the shoulder and swayed in the saddle, desperately gripping his reins with both hands. But then the tearing pain became too much for him, the trees spun around him and a flash of lightning seemed to pierce his head like a sharp golden sword.

He fell from the horse and hit the ground. And then the horse was gone.

The man's fingers scrabbled in the wet grass, then dug into the earth beneath, sinking deeper as, desperately, the man levered himself upwards. He had lost his rifle. He still had his hand-gun. He groped for it, found it, drew it from his holster with his right hand. He was a right-handed man. The bullet had hit him in his shoulder, seemed to have torn a hole right through.

Fighting the pain, he raised himself to his knees, the gun pointing ahead of him. But the long steel barrel was wavering, it was a gleaming steel finger that, in another lightning flash, seemed to be on fire, was a terrible weapon — but it wasn't pointing straight.

Instinctively, he tried to raise his other hand to steady the gun but the claws that worried his shoulder tore at him viciously again and he let the hand flop. His vision was bad. Things moved around him like spectres and the roar of guns was like a thunder he'd never heard before. Never in his life before . . . and he'd been wounded before . . .

Momentarily, he saw the trunk of a tree to the right of him and he leaned towards it, and he made it; he backed against it and tried to raise the gun again and saw the prairie schooner like the battlements of a castle rising before him.

Something smote him in the chest, tearing; it drove him back hard against the tree. "Goldie," said somebody. And there was a man at his side; one of his men. But the face was indistinct. Santono saw a bullet hit the man too, though, thought he heard it. It was a revelation: he'd never heard a bullet hit like that before. A thud, and then a tearing. What terrible things a heavy bullet could do to human flesh!

He saw the man's face then, the eyes staring, the lips twisting. "Goldie," the man whispered and then he fell on his face.

Santono tried to mouth a name, couldn't make it, didn't know whether it was the right name or not. He tried to hold on to the trunk of the tree and it was wet and slimy; he slid around it. He slid down it and it seemed to wrap itself around him and, with a great sigh, he died.

Back at the wagon somebody yelled, "They're running." And so they were. Horsebacked, breaking from the trees, escaping from the blistering fire that had demoralized them, finished some of them, including their leader.

Chase was not practical now, not necessary. The defenders stirred themselves, mixed, took stock. There were no bad wounds among them.

The rain was but a thin drizzle now. It was cooling, almost welcome: they did not protect themselves from it. There was no more lightning and thunder, not even in the distance.

Gabe had a flesh wound in his leg. Dicken bandaged it. Arianne had a cut on her face, didn't know what had caused it. The captive outlaw, unbound now had a nick in his ear where a bullet had creased it. He handed back Lessiter's Winchester. "You did good, son," said this usually taciturn man.

"Folks call me Eddie," said the man. Nobody volunteered to tie him up again.

Ep Swaine came down slowly from the wagon and Simon Klink said, "You shouldn't be doing that."

"I have to," said the young man peevishly, and he walked.

Gabe was sitting on a raised tuft of ground with his bandaged leg held out in front of him. His two friends, Lessiter and Dicken, stood beside him. Swaine went over to them, said, "Jay. I have something to tell you."

There was something about his manner! "Is it a secret?" asked Lessiter sardonically.

"No, I'd like Gabe and Dicken to hear it as well." The younger man kept himself upright, went on quickly, "Before all this started you asked me a question. You asked me why I'd come West. I came here looking for you because you killed my brother and I wanted to kill you. He called himself the Dallas Kid . . . "

"Godamighty," exclaimed old Gabe softly.

"I remember him," said Lessiter. "He threw down on me, got me first. In the shoulder. He was mighty fast, wanted to prove himself the fastest ever. But I got him, got him better. I got him good. I had to . . ."

"We know," put in Dicken. "Jay speaks the truth. He ain't no liar."

"I have to say this, son," said Gabe. "Him bein' your brother an' all. But the Dallas Kid was a notorious no-good."

But Ep Swaine was looking at Lessiter again. And he asked, "Was he really fast?"

"He was one o' the fastest I ever saw."

"He'd like to hear you say that I guess." Ep turned slowly away and Arianne came to him and, her arm around him, led him back to the wagon.

Three outlaws were dead, four counting Ben who had gotten his come-uppance beforehand. One of the other three was Goldie Santono. The bodies were wet and bedraggled and bloody. Simon brought out a lantern and some implements from the wagon and the corpses were made a communal grave with no headstone.

This part was over. But there was yet more to be done and they all knew it. The rain had stopped completely and there was little sound, no alarm. A peaceful night.

23

THEY rolled. They met the posse with Mike Siddens, blacksmith-turned-lawman and young Andy Lugo, whorehouse-attendant-turned-vigilante.

The outlaw called Eddie led them to the hideout by the back way and the folks there were taken by surprise. Two of them were killed and the rest ran like rats, taking their women with them.

The posse were surprised by the look of the camp which was like a small town. They found themselves a rich haul, which would be returned as much as possible to where it came from: outlaw Eddie helped them with information about this. And there was the express office loot from the distant town of Raylondo.

Eddie was given a small poke to

tide him on his way and, warily, he went in a different direction to the one taken by the fugitives from the hideout. Marshal Lessiter said threateningly that he didn't ever want to see Eddie's face again. Eddie said he'd make sure o' that all right, and he meant it.

Riding his own horse away from there and, after putting a fair distance between himself and the hills, Eddie looked back and saw the column of black smoke rising into the morning sky.

The posse had fired the place, which was the best thing to do with it, the end of it. Eddie gave a small thought to his dead ex-partner, Ben, and blessed his own rude health — except for a bullet-torn ear which itched but was mending nicely — and was glad to be free, and still in the land of the living. He hadn't the recklessness and aggression in his make-up that had characterized his friend, Ben, so maybe he'd try to go straight now — stranger things had happened and that was a fact.

He waved a hand at the hills behind and imagined that the folks there were waving back at him. Lessiter, Dicken, Gabe, the professor, the two lovely girls, the young Easterner who was mending well: good folks to carry with him in his mind . . .

★ ★ ★

Andy still had his tattered old ledger tucked under his arm. This made for a little difficulty with the reins of his horse; but the young bucko didn't seem to want to let the precious book go, not even stashed away in his saddle-bag.

"What you got there, son?" Dicken asked.

"I was kinda wondering about that," put in Lessiter.

Andy looked from one to the other of them as if trying to make up his mind about something.

Then he said, "I'm going to write a book about all this. About that stinking *bandido*, Goldie Santono, and no hero-worship for that one. No, sir! But about you too, Marshal, and about Bess and me, and Big Mike, and the professor and the girls, and Dicken and Gabe and all the rest. I'll make us all famous, you see if I don't."

"Stranger things have happened I guess," said Marshal Jay Lessiter.

"An' that's a fact all right," said Emmy Dicken laconically.

THE END